Billy Thomas

FOREVER FEARLESS

Billy Thomas

FOREVER FEARLESS

David Carlyle

Mill City Press, Minneapolis

Mill City Press, Inc.
322 First Avenue N, 5th floor
Minneapolis, MN 55401
612.455.2293
www.millcitypublishing.com

ISBN-13: 978-1-63413-249-7
LCCN: 2014921812

Book design by Lois Stanfield

Printed in the United States of America

CHAPTER ONE

The Wagon Wreck

March 1899

YOUNG BILLY THOMAS knew his horses could kill him the instant they spooked, but he didn't worry at first; he'd soothed terrified horses before, and he expected to calm these. His mom described him as "fearless, rebellious, and stupid," to her neighbors and church friends. She even claimed she used those exact words in a letter to her sister back east somewhere. He didn't think the word "stupid" fit him at all, and he didn't want to be stupid this time. He felt pride in the "fearless" part of his mom's picture and agreed with the "rebellious" part only because he thought he had to rebel against her sometimes to fill his role as leader of his family, a job he didn't want, but forced on him when his dad died suddenly over two years earlier. He'd fearlessly crawled under his mom's house last summer when she thought she heard a wolf under it. But to avoid being stupid, he didn't shoot the skunk he found there. He fearlessly climbed to the top of his barn and his mom's barn before hay season each year, to thread the hay rope through pulleys wired up there. And again because he didn't want to be stupid, he used care as he ascended and descended.

His horses spooked after they pulled an iron-wheeled wagon with a box on it filled with oats, over most of a small field next to Thomas Creek, and Billy threw, or broadcast, the oats on the field on his Joaquin County, Missouri farm. The horses, a mottled brown and white gelding named Brownie and a black and white spotted gelding called Spot, jumped and ran when a blue heron swooped low over them and croaked. They threw up their heads, stuck their tails straight out behind, and turned toward the creek along the west edge of the small field. Billy realized he couldn't stop them until they ran themselves down, but thought, either fearlessly or stupidly, he could turn them. He couldn't. So he stood to his full height of five feet, eight inches, and pulled straight back on the 'lines,' as he called them, with all his considerable strength in a last desperate effort to stop; he didn't expect it to work, but held on too long to jump before the right front wagon wheel hit a four-inch hickory tree adjacent to the creek. Billy didn't jump, but momentum carried him forward, and he fell between the wagon and the horses. Bark loosened and slipped off the tree, the wagon wheel slid left around it after only a very short pause, and the horses ran on into and across the creek. He quickly rolled a full turn to his left, made himself as flat on his belly as he could, and watched both front wagon wheels pass beside him. One of the rear wheels he couldn't see, ran over his right leg, his back, his left shoulder, and moved him forward a few inches to cause a crunching sound in his back and to put his face under water in the creek. He felt the box fall on both his lower legs, but he tried to move after only a moment, because he knew if he could possibly do it, he had to roll over to get his nose or mouth out of the water.

He tried to roll but the wagon box prevented it, and the pain, especially in his back, made him think he might pass out. He held his breath as long as he could, then lifted his head a couple inches, and grabbed a quick breath before he allowed his head to fall back into the water. He continued that as long as he could, and used his mind while partly in the water, because he could use almost no other body part. He thought of Robert, and felt regret because he knew Robert couldn't fully protect and provide for his family. Just before fatigue and pain caused his world to go dark, he accepted the "stupid" label, and realized he should have jumped from the wagon while he still could. He didn't know about it, but his face presumably remained in the water.

Billy awakened in his bed in the middle room of his mom's three-rooms-in-a-row house. It had a ten by ten kitchen on the west, with the only door to the outside there, on the south, another ten by ten room in the middle, with a third ten by ten on the east. He saw young Doctor Chisholm and Janet Thomas, his mom, standing beside the bed, and saw his three younger brothers, plus Ron Knight, a neighbor from the other side of the creek, standing near the foot of the bed. All looked at him with obvious concern, and Ron, a middle-aged but fit farmer, explained, "I come a runnin' when I seen them horses a pullin' your wagon without no box outta' the woods. I don't think you'd o' lasted much longer."

Janet gave a tight little smile to Ron. "Thank goodness you did. I don't want to lose Billy. After losing Steve, it would nearly kill me."

Ron replied, "It nearly *did* kill Billy."

Billy moved his eyes to see everybody in the room. Ron sported a trimmed beard, blue overalls, a blue work shirt, and a straw hat he'd neglected to take off. Janet, Billy's short, pretty, and only slightly chubby mom had light brown hair barely below her ears, with reading glasses on top. She wore a green dress with white flowers on it, and with white buttons down the front. She made it herself from feed sacks, and it covered her from her neck to her ankles. His brothers were ten-, eight-, and seven-years-old, stair stepped, each with sandy-blond hair, and dressed in blue overalls and blue shirts like both Billy and Ron. Dr. Chisholm's un-tanned face and arms didn't seem to fit with the others'. Billy tried to move his feet; he thought maybe he could do it, but the severe pain made him stop. He tried to talk, but even to open his mouth made his back hurt. He settled for a weak smile.

Doctor Chisholm, smooth-faced and tall with wide shoulders, dressed in a blue and green sport shirt and tan slacks, looked down at Billy's mom and said, "He's come to; that's good; he didn't break any bones, and that's good too. I'll go now, but Billy'll be real sore for a few days. Make sure he moves around as much and as soon as he can. You send for me if anything changes, you hear?" Dr. Chisholm went out the door, climbed into his buggy, clucked to his horse, turned the buggy around, drove out the driveway past the kitchen end of the house, and turned northeast on the road back to Fiskur.

Billy's mom tried to feed him and help him drink; he didn't want food or water but couldn't speak or move, so she continued for a short time. The food and water dribbled out the sides of his mouth. Robert, Billy's oldest brother, told him he'd feed the animals and milk Bessie the cow until Billy could do it again. Billy's eyes went to Robert, and he noted how mature, muscular, and grown-up Robert looked for a not much over four-foot ten-year-old. Robert helped him with farm work, hunted with him, fished with him, and occasionally fed the live-stock for him. Billy realized—again, for about the hundredth time—he could never take care of his mom and younger brothers without Robert. But he also knew Robert couldn't do it alone.

Ron stuck his thumbs under his overalls galluses and said, "I gotta go, Miz Thomas, but I'll find them horses o' your'n, bring'em back, put the box back on the wagon, and put ever'thing away." He said over his shoulder to Billy as he left, "You git better quick, Son, ya hear?"

Billy smiled. He remained silent and motionless as his mom sat with him all the rest of that day and night. He thought about his dad, Steve Thomas, the former leader of the family. He'd died suddenly over two years ago, to leave a big hole in the Thomas family. His dad gave the Joaquin County farm to Billy on his fifteenth birthday. He re-membered the ugly argument with his mom when she didn't want him to drop out of school in April after his dad died in October, and how he didn't want to be in school anyway, especially because Susan had skipped a couple grades and would soon have a diploma. He thought about Susan during that day and night also, the beautiful girl he once intended to propose marriage to after her eighteenth birthday, around a couple months away. But now he didn't know if he'd recover enough to be a decent husband for an active and vivacious girl like Susan.

Billy smelled the bacon and biscuits his mom cooked for breakfast the next morning, and felt hungry. He moved his feet a bit, but his back hurt too much to get out of bed. He tried to talk, and his speech seemed normal. He asked for food, and his mom fed him.

"Thanks, Mom, that was real good."

"I'm glad you could enjoy it Son. When Ron dragged you in here yesterday, I didn't know if you'd ever be able to eat again. I'm thrilled you can."

Billy tried to look tough—no easy task while in bed, not able to feed himself—but did the best he could. "I'm stronger'n you think, Mom." His mom smiled and made a dismissive wave in his direction.

Billy hobbled around in the house three days later, on Saturday. He fished for a yes, as he asked, "You think I'll be able to go out and do the chores tonight, Mom?"

He didn't get the yes. "Look at yourself, Son. You can barely walk. I hope you get better, but you're not there yet. No, you can't go tonight."

"You think tomorrow night?"

"I don't know how fast you'll get better, Billy, or *if* you'll get better. But tomorrow night's out of the question. No, not tomorrow night."

Billy tried to return to bed, but eventually had to ask Robert to help him. After Robert endured some criticism including, "Don't push me like a sack of feed," "You're rushin' me," and more, he made it.

Janet took the younger boys to church Sunday, and he practiced while they were away. He got out of bed himself and back in twice before his family returned. He remained in bed and said nothing until his mom called the younger boys to dinner. Then he said, "I think I can make it to the table today, Mom."

Janet frowned. "You better not, Son. I'll bring your food again."

Billy responded by getting out of bed. It hurt, but he tried to hide the pain and to make it look easy. He then walked to the kitchen table, pulled out a chair and sat in it. As before, he tried to make it look easy. Janet worried, "Are you sure you ought to be up, Son?"

"Didn't Dr. Chisholm say for me to move around as soon as I can?"

"Well, he did, but . . .

"So I'm doing it. Aren't you glad about that?"

"Maybe in a way, but I worry you'll break something, and end your walking chances forever."

He did his morning chores on Monday, albeit a bit later than normal. He thanked all his brothers, "Thanks Robert, and thanks Ed and Timmy, for filling in for me. I appreciate it, and don't know how the animals would have made it without you. I did it this morning, though, and think I can take the job back. It hurt—a lot—but still it felt good to actually do something. Thank you again." Tough Robert looked embarrassed. Skinny Ed, and little Timmy knew Robert did all the work, but grinned anyway.

Billy planned to finish the oat seeding at his farm Thursday, and to seed oats on his mom's farm Friday, the last day of March. He did both, and didn't feel undue pain, except when his mom chastised him Thursday. She verbally jumped on him the instant he came through the door. "Where have you been all this time?"

"I been sowing oats."

"What! That's how you got hurt in the first place."

"Yeah. Do you want me to just sit in the house the rest of my days?"

"Well, at least for a while. You don't want to hurt your back again before it even heals."

Billy put his hands as close to the floor as he could make them go. "It's healed, Mom. Look."

"Well, if you say so. But be really careful, and stay away from those horses for at least another few months."

"I sowed oats on my place today. I plan to sow on your place tomorrow. It'll be too late in another few months."

"Oh Billy, you're way too headstrong for your own good."

"Whatever you say, Mom, but the dirt's right, and I gotta sow those oats tomorrow."

Janet turned away. Billy grabbed the milk bucket off the table and went back outside. He realized he didn't understand how his mom thought, but expected to feel fine by mid-May, in time to plant corn on both farms. He didn't plan to sell oats or corn, but to augment last year's straw barns at both farms, and to feed grain to the sow and pigs, chickens, and horses at his farm, and to Bessie at his mom's farm. Brownie and Spot were his dad's horses, but when he died, Billy claimed them along with the wagon and harness and most of his dad's tools, including his single-shot .22 rifle. He moved those to his farm.

He planned to paint the outside of his mom's house and then his newly vacant house on the Joaquin County farm, starting the first Monday in April. His mom's house, south of Fiskur at the edge of Sinfe County, stood only about a hundred yards from his, a little farther south across the Joaquin County line. The road from Fiskur to the north, ran mostly south, but jogged southwest just north of his mom's house, then turned south again beside her house, and went south all the way to Shawsville, several miles south of Billy's house. Janet's driveway went north and intersected the road barely northeast of the curve back to the south. The Knight's driveway, at a right angle to the north-south part of the road between Billy's house and his mom's, but north of Billy's, crossed Thomas creek on a little bridge and continued west up and over the creek bluff for a total of another sixty yards or so. The driveway went between the Knight's barn on the south and their house on the north. Billy's short driveway, parallel to the Knight's, went south of his house and ended in front of his barn.

His mom's twenty-something-year-old house sat on a rock foundation, but had never been painted. He thought he'd need to paint at least three coats, counting a primer. His house, an older two-room structure, also on a rock foundation, showed traces of paint, but he decided it needed as much paint as the other house. He wanted to do it soon, now that Old Man Clarkson had moved out of it and into Fiskur, but before he asked Susan to marry him. He informed his mother, "Mom, I plan to paint your house early next week, and to begin mine later in the week."

His mom shook her head. Her brown eyes were not hidden behind the reading glasses atop her head; they blazed, and she raised her voice. "Billy, this house doesn't need paint. It's never been painted, and looks like a palace to me. Your father and I moved into it before you were born; we liked it then, and I like it now."

"Have you noticed the rot that's starting around the edges of all the siding boards? Paint will make them last a lot longer."

"But you're not well enough to work like that."

"You'll never say I'm well enough! But if I don't start to work sometime, I'll end up a lazy loafer."

His mom stamped her foot and frowned. "I forbid you to do it."

"I was eighteen years old last November. I'll do it if I want to, and I do."

She frowned again, then said with as much authority as she could, "But I'm your mother."

"That's exactly why I plan to do it!"

Her fight seemed to evaporate. "Well, if you must, but if you get even a little bit tired, promise me you'll stop."

"Since I'm the only one who'll know, a promise won't mean much."

His mom recovered her fight. "Billy, I don't ever want to see you like you were last week."

"Horses made me that way, not paint."

"A lot of things can make you that way; I was little at the time, but I still remember survivors of the Battle of Lone Jack. I don't want you to end up like they did."

"I'll be fine, and I'll paint."

Billy hitched Brownie and Spot to the wagon again after break-fast on April Fool's Day, and drove to Fiskur to buy five gallons of Cutler and Neilson Paint Primer, plus ten gallons of regular paint. His back throbbed and hurt when he arrived, but he knew no way to get home except to ride the wagon back.

When he returned, he took the wagon behind the barn and tried to minimize obvious reaction to his pain. His mom asked when he entered the house, "Where'd you go?"

"Fiskur."

"Fiskur? How'd you hold up?"

"All right."

"Does your back hurt?"

"Not much."

"Why'd you go?"

"To get paint."

"Oh."

When Billy took the horses and wagon behind the barn south of the house, he didn't unhitch or unload paint immediately, because his back hurt too much. He came back after his noon meal and did those things, but with pain and great care.

He put primer on his mom's house on Monday and felt tired but not much pained. He could have worked three more hours, but stopped. He painted a topcoat on Tuesday and another on Wednes-day. His mom exclaimed over how much better the house looked, and dropped her objections to Billy's work. He worked at the same pace at his house, finished by noon on Saturday, and had paint left over.

CHAPTER TWO

Shootings at the Barn

April 1899

BILLY FELT FINE when he finished painting, and made plans for interior work at his house to begin on Monday. His house already had a wood-burning heating stove in the sitting/sleeping room on the east and a cook stove in the kitchen on the west, so he didn't have a lot to do. He wanted to update the bed in his house with springs, to build a pie safe for the kitchen, and to make a second chair to sit on. But when he walked down the road ready to enter the house and to begin, he noticed the middle door open on his barn, southwest of the house. He went to the barn to shut the door, and heard voices as he approached. He didn't close the door, but yelled, "Hello! Anybody in there?"

In answer, a bullet whizzed by his ear. Although Billy had a single-shot rifle, he didn't have it in his hands. He ran for the cover of a big cedar tree between the house and barn, waited there a few minutes, then slowly backed up in line with the tree, until he could break for the east side of the house. His break didn't draw another shot, so he circled north among trees, to a spot where he could almost see both east and west barn doors; the barn didn't have doors on the north or south. He saw two saddled mares, a black and a bay, tied behind the barn on the west but saw no people, waited for a while, and went back among trees to his mom's house for lunch. Along the way, he considered whether to tell his mom about the shot at him, but decided against

11

it; he thought he shouldn't worry her. He kept a close eye on windows during lunch, but saw nothing unususal, and talked little. He returned to his hiding place on the Joaquin County farm immediately after his meal, looked for the horses, and saw them tied as before. He didn't want to waste the entire day, but didn't know what else to do, so he crept up to the north wall of the barn, listened, heard voices, and then ran back to his hiding spot. He felt glad he had his dad's rifle, but then remembered he kept it in the barn, near the east door.

He waited in his hiding spot until he formed a plan; he approached the barn again, heard voices again as he stood at the north wall, waited a couple minutes, moved around front and grabbed his rifle. He drew another harmless shot as he did, but hustled back to his hiding spot north of the barn. He settled down to wait but then realized his rifle shells were in a manger near where the rifle had been. So he repeated his grabbing maneuver, actually got a handful of shells, but heard another bullet go by, then quickly felt one hit his achy shoulder. He ran back to the trees north of the barn and pulled his shirt back. He saw the bullet only cut into his outer arm, and realized he'd live. He wrapped his handkerchief around his arm to soak up the blood, put a shell in the rifle, and waited more. Nothing happened during the first few minutes, so he counted his shells. He had four and decided to waste one. He moved to an open place west of his hiding spot, shot at the barn's north wall, then jumped back to his hiding place behind trees. He grinned, and thought to himself he could indeed hit the broad side of a barn! After a short interval two men, one a little older than his dad, big, fat, gray-bearded, and tall, the other a bit younger, short, smooth-faced, and skinny, both with old and bent felt hats, ran out the west barn door. They jumped on the horses, and rode south to a fence, then west along the fence. Billy thought he could have shot them, but instead he yelled, "Don't you ever come back!" He worried they might, and maybe soon.

He'd only seen two mares, then saw two men, but decided to go check the barn anyway. He entered the east door with caution, crept all the way past two horse stalls, tried to tiptoe past his chicken enclosure but jumped sideways when a chicken cackled and flew, walked more confidently past a crib, and out the west door opposite the east one. He found nobody, so he went back and picked up his remaining two shells, He took everything to his mom's house. He showed her his shoulder, told what happened, and didn't go back until the next day.

His mom cleaned and bandaged the shoulder, and then nagged him. "Don't you go back near that barn or house, ever."

"What good is it if I let people scare me away from it? Do you want me to hide in your house until I rot?" Billy felt anxious the two guys might come back, but didn't want his mom to know.

Janet ignored the second question. "Maybe it's no good at all, but which is worth more, your life or your farm?"

"My life's worthless if I live too much in fear. I've got my rifle now, and don't feel as defenseless as I did."

"I know you. You said 'Amen' just yesterday in church, when Pastor Javier said we must forgive our enemies. You won't shoot anybody."

"Maybe, maybe not. But they'll have to wonder if I will or won't."

"They'll shoot first and wonder later."

"They'd better do it in the other order if they know what's good for them." He felt he had to appear fearless to his mom, and couldn't let her know his concern the men might return.

Billy went back to his house on Tuesday, saw no horses and heard no voices, but walked all the way around the barn and then through it, before he went into the house. Everything seemed in order, so he went to work in the house. He heard a horse approach after a couple hours or so. He picked up his loaded rifle, went out to see the short skinny man he'd seen the day before, on the same black mare, and immediately wondered about the location of the tall fat guy. He pointed the rifle at the skinny man, tried to keep his voice steady and firm, and said, "Your partner'd better not try to come up behind me, because if I see him, I shoot you."

13

The skinny guy answered, "It was Zach that shot at you yesterday. I don't have a gun and didn't know he had one. I came to apologize and to tell you I'm done with Zach and won't bother you again."

"I don't believe that for a minute, but just know that if you come back, you're dead. Back your horse up, ride out of here fast, and if your fat friend doesn't show up before you're out of range, I'll let you live for a while." The short person left in a hurry. Billy took the rifle, looked around and in the barn again, and around and in the house. He saw nothing, but had a hunch both guys would someday return. He kept the loaded rifle close. When he thought it might be near noon, he took the rifle, headed to his mom's house, and saw smoke before he saw the house. He started to run and saw the house on fire, but then saw his mom and his three brothers outside. Billy continued to run until he came close enough to yell, "You guys all right?"

His mom and two younger brothers started to cry. Robert did too, but talked through his tears. "A big guy came up here, said he'd shoot us all, went to the barn and got hay, put it by the house, and set it on fire. We all came out and he didn't shoot us, but my stick horse is in there."

"I'll make you another stick horse. I'm just glad we have another house. I think we'll abandon this one for a while—we don't have a choice, it's about gone—we'll take the animals except for the chickens to my farm, keep an eye on the barn here as much as we can, and maybe someday we can rebuild this house. First I have to find the big guy."

CHAPTER THREE

Search for the Big Guy

April 1899

BILLY ASKED, "Which way'd he go?"

His mom's face turned white. "Who go?"

"The big guy with the matches."

"Billy, you're not going near that man. You're going to stay here where it's safe. I just begrudge every minute you spent putting paint on the house; all that's wasted now."

"Some safety. Weren't you here?"

"I was here. That's why you can't go."

Billy grinned. He said, "Well, I can go and must go, but that's not why I don't want to go. Although Susan visited me while I was down, I went too long without seeing her. And unless I find Big Fats quick, I'll go too long again!"

"You're off your rocker if Susan is all you worry about."

"Mom, Susan *isn't* the only person I worry about. I'm afraid for you and the boys. If I don't find the guy who burned the house, he'll be back. And we don't know what he might do on a return trip. I do know we can't go down to my farm, hole up, and hide until we're all old. I gotta' lay down the law to him, and quick. Are you gonna tell me which way he went, or not?"

"I'm not."

"Then I'll have to track him from the beginning."

Robert spoke up. "He went out the driveway to the road on a bay, and turned northeast on the road jog."

"Oh, no! A horse or wagon goes on that road almost every day. I'll never be able to see his tracks in the road, even though we did have a little shower on Monday. I'll have to follow him around the jog, then north, and hope to see where he left the road, if he did. I also don't want to be gone a long time in case he comes back. We'll all go down to my house, I'll make sure everything's all right there, and if it is, I'll come back and try to find the guy. I wish I had two rifles, so I could leave one with you."

Billy's mom answered, "We wouldn't know what to do with a rifle if we had one. You don't either. You should throw yours in the creek, and stay home with us."

Billy ignored his mom's comment. "Let's go to the other house. There's nothing to move except animals, so all we have to do is walk down there. Then I'll go, and hope to get back tonight or tomorrow. I'll move all the animals except the chickens, after that. The chicken part of my barn's already full."

They went to the other house, Billy checked the inside and the barn again, then went back north. The dirt around his mom's house revealed a little notch in the left front bay horseshoe, so maybe he'd be able to track the mare after all. He walked around the still smoldering house a moment to look for other clues; he didn't find more, so he went out to the road and followed the notched shoe. Billy walked until near sundown, then lost the notched shoe. He went back and found where the shoe went off the road on the left side, near another barn.

He approached the barn straight on from the east, looked through the open upper half of a horse door, and saw a bay horse in a stall inside. He ran around the south side of the barn to the west side, saw no doors there, came back to the south side, and stopped a moment to think. He decided to wait until dark, take the presumed mare out of the barn, run her off, and then try to find the man in the barn. He sat down to wait, with his back against the barn and his rifle across his knees. He waited until he could barely see the outline of a tree south of the barn, then crawled on his hands and knees around to the east. He opened the bottom half of the door, crawled inside, and left the door open. He crawled to the mare's head, stood, quietly untied the her, slapped her on the rump, yelled, and jumped behind a board partition in the barn. She ran out the barn door, galloped east, and a bullet ripped through a board just over his head. He fell flat and tried to guess where the bullet came from. Soon a couple more sprayed the area, and he determined they came from the loft—probably accessible in only one way. He crawled partly under a hay manger, watched the ladder to the loft, and waited. He saw the outline of a man on the ladder after about an hour.

He jumped up, pointed his rifle at the man's back, and said, "I got you now. You think it's fun to terrorize an innocent woman and her children? How about an armed man? Is your buddy still up in the loft?" Billy all but knew the big guy came in the barn alone, because he found only one mare and one set of tracks.

The man almost whimpered. "Don't shoot. I ain't got no buddy; he took off. I'll never bother you again if you won't shoot."

"Don't come any farther down the ladder. I need some time to decide whether to shoot. But if you move, that'll make up my mind quick."

Billy allowed about two minutes to go by. Then, "You got your gun on you?"

"No, don't shoot me."

"Where is it?"

"Up in the hay."

"I don't believe you."

"Don't shoot. It's up there. Don't shoot me, please."

"Move down the ladder slow, then walk out of the barn slow. You make a fast move and I shoot. You don't know exactly where I'm at, so you don't know exactly where to shoot. But I can see you, and I know where."

"Don't shoot. I'll come down, slow."

"See that you do."

The man came gingerly down the ladder, and moved out into a less dark place in front of the door. Billy recognized him as the person he expected, and said, "Now walk up to the house and knock on the door. We'll talk to the feller inside a bit. Don't forget I'm right behind you with a rifle aimed at your backbone."

The man walked a few steps, then stopped. "Don't shoot. Just let me go. I don't wanna talk to the feller inside."

"You want me to shoot you?"

"No . . . no, never."

"Then start walking again, up to the door and knock."

The man walked all the way to the door, but didn't knock. "Why cain't you just let me go. If you shoot, you'll likely shoot somebody inside."

"I got a little rifle. You'll stop the bullet—it won't go all the way through. Now knock."

The guy knocked, the door opened, and Billy spoke to the man inside. "I found this person in your barn. He's a criminal, but he's on your property, for you to decide about."

"You know for sure he's a criminal?"

"Yep."

"I'll take'im out to the barn and tie'im to a post. I'll talk to'im in the mornin' and decide whether to take'im to the sheriff in Riverbeach."

"He's a really bad guy. Maybe somebody ought to watch him and keep a gun on him all night."

"I can tie'im so he won't get away, but if you want to watch'im, you're welcome to it."

"What if you tie him outside, to a tree, where it's less dark?"

"That's all right by me." The man tied the big guy to a tree in his yard, patted him down, took two pistols out of his pocket, and said, "Looks like you're right when you say he's a bad guy."

Billy nodded and sat down to watch. He expected the man to try to get away, but he sat quietly and eventually went to sleep. Billy struggled with sleep early; he didn't know why, but he grew a bit stronger after the man fell asleep. The bearded guy remained at daybreak when the man inside opened the door. "You wanta come in for breakfast?"

"No, I don't want to let this guy think nobody's watching him."

"Suit yourself." The man came out after a few minutes, hitched two horses to a wagon, threw a post into it, and tied the big guy to the post.

The man then asked, "What's your name? Where you live?"

"Billy Thomas. Six hours walk south of here, down in Joaquin County. What's your name?"

"Ben Wilson. I'uz about to offer you a ride, but you live pretty far off the road to Riverbeach. It's not more'n a hop, skip, and a jump from here."

"I followed him here on foot. I can get back the same way."

The man drove toward Riverbeach with the criminal in his wagon, and Billy started toward home. He hoped never to see the big guy again, but realized he'd always be concerned about it.

CHAPTER FOUR

Susan

April 1899

BILLY RETURNED TO HIS HOME in time for a late lunch on Wednesday—a scanty one, because his mom's food supplies burned in her former house. His mom's face, however, showed an almost continuous smile and a hint of mystery. She made the hint verbal near the end of Billy's lunch. "Are you going to ask who dropped by here for a visit today?"

Billy crammed the last of his food into his mouth. "Who?"

"She's somebody you know."

Billy instantly knew who, so asked, "Why'd she visit?"

"She wanted to see if we're all right."

"Did she ask about me?"

His mom grinned big. "Why do you ask?"

Billy's face showed mild irritation. "Did she?"

"Of course she did! She's a wonderful Christian girl, and you're lucky you know her."

Billy grinned. "I know I'm lucky. If she had three sisters, I'd want Robert, Ed, and Timmy to marry them all. After I married Susan, of course!"

"You'd better not let Susan hear you talk about anybody besides her!"

"She won't. And don't tell her what I said."

"Maybe I should. I'm afraid I already disobey the commandment about giving false testimony! My only defense is the commandment says we must not give false testimony *against*. But I give false testimony to Susan regularly. I tell her you're a fine boy." She grinned.

Billy held back an answering grin. "Can't you tell her I'm a fine *man?*"

His mom, still grinning, replied, "There's a limit to how false I want to be."

Billy shook his head. "Mom, I love you, but you're hopeless." He went out his door, walked around to the west of the house, and went into the barn to plan a new house for his mom. Now that the big guy might be in custody, he thought it safe to build it, but first he had to cut logs and get them to the sawmill a couple miles south. He sat in the barn a few minutes, decided to build a gable-roofed house like the old one, with three ten by ten rooms as before, but to close in the front porch to make a second sleeping room, eight by twelve. He figured if he kept the same footprint, he could build on the existing foundation. He grabbed his one-man saw off two nails in the barn wall, and headed for the woods by the creek. He worked only until midafternoon, then went back to his house, washed his face and hands, and asked his mom, "You want to go into Fiskur tomorrow to buy food or clothes or anything? Me and the boys are sleeping on the floor, you know, because our beds burned in the other house. I don't want to make more beds until I can make them for your new house, but you might want other stuff."

"That's a thoughtful thing, Billy, but I don't have much money now. Maybe after I sell a few more eggs and fryers I can do it. The egg case is only about half full now, but it could go to Fiskur sometime next week."

"I'll take it whenever you say. Right now I think I'll call on Susan."

"Don't you want to wait and eat your supper first?"

"No, maybe Susan's mom'll have something."

"That's not polite, Billy, to show up just before suppertime."

"I'm leaving now. I might get home late."

"Well, all right. Bye."

Billy went out the door and slammed it. He started out his driveway and saw a six-wagon caravan approach; it turned out to be from South Sinfe County Church, up the road north about a mile. Each wagon had food in it. Susan's parents, Mary and Earl Kovachovich, brought a couple bushels of potatoes, some flour, and some sugar. Mary looked like an older version of her petite daughter, Susan, but big, tall, heavy, goateed, and sweaty Earl didn't look at all like her. Ron and Gertrude Knight brought more potatoes, corn ground fine into corn meal, and two gallons of molasses. Ron and 'Gertie' looked remarkably the same; a few years older than the Kovachaviches, short, tanned, lean, and fit. Other people brought lard, oatmeal, canned meats and vegetables, and a dozen live fryers, along with fifty pounds of store-bought chicken feed. Susan didn't come, so when everyone left, Billy walked north up the road roughly two miles to her house. Susan opened the door to him and came out on the little front porch. He looked down at her from his height a couple inches taller, and said, "Hi, Beautiful." She truly did look beautiful, with her blue eyes, slightly up-turned nose, perfect skin, and lacy dress.

Susan tossed her lovely brownish-blonde hair, blushed, and answered, "Hello yourself, handsome."

Billy knew the word 'handsome' didn't describe him, not only because of the dirty clothes he couldn't change because the fire burned the others, but also because of his too-flat nose, his shaggy reddish blonde hair—not a beautiful color like Susan's, but his looked more like a dirty mess—his still-stiff and off-level shoulder, and a dozen or so freckles on his face, mixed with a few shallow chicken pox scars. But when Susan used the word, he grinned and accepted it. He bent down and gave her a quick kiss on her cheek; she said, "That's no good," reached up, put her arms around his neck, pulled him down, and kissed him on the lips. She didn't let go for at least a half minute. Then she said, "Come on in. I have a surprise for you."

She led him to the table in the center of the little one-room house, and showed him two pairs of new overalls, two new shirts, a pair of new pants, and suspenders.

Billy didn't understand. "What's this stuff for?"

Susan seemed taken aback until her mom said, "Tell him, Susan."

She said, "For you. I made it all, except for the suspenders, from feed sacks and from Daddy's old overalls. He put on so much weight he had to have new."

It was Billy's turn to be taken aback. "Wow! I didn't know you could do stuff like this. Wow!"

Susan grinned and lit up the room with her even and beautiful teeth. "You'd be surprised at what I can do. Why don't you go behind the hanging blanket in the corner, put new overalls on, and sit down to a meal Mom and I made."

"How'd you know I'd be here tonight?"

"Well, I didn't know for sure, but I hoped you would, and I thought it possible."

"I'm free during the early evening for a good long while. I'll make the change, and a meal sure will hit the spot."

Billy ate as if he'd never seen food before. He didn't talk all through the meal, but merely stared at Susan's womanly form and enjoyed the food. When finished, he complimented, "That sure was good. Mr. Kovachovich, you're a lucky man!"

Mrs. Kovachovich answered, "Susan baked the pies and fried the chicken. I just made the salad and mashed the pototoes."

"Either way, Mr. Kovachovich, you're the luckiest man I know. I hope Susan will make me as lucky as you some day."

Susan's dad smiled. "If you ask Susan right now, I bet she'll say yes."

Billy turned fiery red, but said, "Susan, I intended to wait to ask you until after your birthday, but with an invitation like your dad just made, I have to do it now. I love you, Susan. Will you marry me?"

Susan didn't seem to need time to think. She exclaimed, "Yes!"

Billy apologized, "I don't have a ring, but maybe I'll have one by the time we can marry. I have to build a house for Mom and keep up with the farm work, but you can know I'll do it all as fast as I can. You want to go for a walk outside?"

Susan's dad winked at her mother, and said, "Mary and I want to walk outside. Why don't you kids have the house this evening?"

Susan answered, "We'll love it. How soon can you be gone!?"

Her dad replied, "We're on our way out the door now. We'll be gone exactly an hour." He pulled out his pocket watch, looked at it, put it back, and they left

Billy had an overpowering and irresistible urge to kiss Susan. He grabbed her, held her tight, and kissed. She didn't resist. After the kiss, they sat on chairs facing each other, and looked at each other for several minutes. Susan broke the silence. "I'm not much of a man, but I'll help build your mom's house."

Billy grinned. "You got that right. You're not much of a man! But I'll welcome you any time you can come—not to work like a man, but to decorate the area. You don't in any way look like a man, so I'll kiss you again!"

They kissed, kissed again, and then a few more times, before Susan went back to the earlier conversation. "No, I mean it . . . Should we set a date for a wedding?"

"I hope we can set a date real soon, for a time also real soon, but maybe we should hold off at aleast until I get the logs cut, so we'll know better when the house'll be done. I want to do a little work at our house too."

"Our house doesn't need work, or if it does, it will be something you can do in the winter after we're married."

"Well, I'm easy convinced about that. But I must cut logs. I'll cut every day except Sundays, rain or shine, and maybe I'll have enough by the end of April. What's the exact day you'll be eighteen?"

"That's splendid, Billy. I'm sure my dad can round up a bunch of men to build the house in only days. I'll be eighteen on Thursday, May 4, but I don't see a need to wait that long."

"I don't see a need either, but I can't build the house that fast. It's nice to know we can marry as soon as it's done, though."

"Let's just sit here until Mom and Dad come back. I want to look at you some more."

"Oh, Susan, not half as bad as I want to look at you."

They sat in silence for over a minute, kissed for another ten, then Susan talked up a storm about wedding details. She continued to talk until her parents returned. Billy commented to the older Kovachoviches, "I better get home and rest. I want to work a lot tomorrow and every day, but if you want to get rid of Susan in the evenings, send her over. I want nothing so much as to entertain her! If she isn't at my house by the end of suppertime, I'll be here at your house soon after, and she'll have to entertain me! Better yet, Susan, why don't you come over for lunch every day, and we can decide then who visits who that evening?"

"I'll be there every day at lunch! Tell your mom I'll bring dessert each time."

Billy cut logs every day. Earl Kovachovich, Ron Knight, and two other guys came every day also, except the second Thursday and Friday in April, when it rained. They not only cut logs, they helped haul to and from the sawmill; they were ready to build more than two full weeks before Susan's birthday. Ron told Billy, "Me and Earl and four other guys'll show up on Friday to start the house. If'n we cain't build it in a week, you oughta shoot us all. Then me and three guys'll show up Saturday after, t' make furniture, and'll be back on Thursday afternoon late, to help Janet and th' boys move in. Thursday night, April 20, Billy and Susan set a date to marry; Sunday afternoon, May 7. He walked all the way to Fiskur on Saturday, May 6, to buy a ring.

Billy might have taken more care with a few building details if he'd done the house himself, but he appreciated the help and the speed. His mom and brothers moved on the expected day, in a light rain most of the time, and Susan visited for a few minutes after her dad went home. Billy asked, "Can you come over tomorrow? I'll ask Robert to chaperone us, and we can go down to our house and fix it up."

"Sure. It'll be fun! What time?"

"How about seven-thirty?"

Billy slept in his mom's house for one of the last times, and Susan arrived the next morning. The two of them and Robert walked down to the Joaquin County home. Susan cleaned every speck of dust out of the kitchen, added curtains to each of the two windows that day, and both Robert and Billy enjoyed the 'meal out of a basket' she brought; the two boys worked mostly outside in the yard.

Billy looked at his pocket watch in the later afternoon, then looked at Susan. "Uh-oh. It's five-thirty already. We'd probably better go as soon as it gets dark, because I have a few chores, both here and at Mom's place, and your folks might start to worry if you get home too late."

They worked a bit longer, ate another 'meal out of a basket', and Billy noted, "It's starting to get dark. We'd better go in a couple of minutes." He found his hat, put it on, and asked, "You have a hat, Robert?" After a no, he asked Susan, "You ready to go?" He planned to walk with Susan and Robert to his mom's home, then to continue and to walk Susan home. But none of that happened. The short guy on the black mare Billy had encountered in his barn rode out of the road and almost to them, before they came to the halfway point in the driveway. He pointed a gun at Billy and said, "That's a mighty fine lookin' girl you got there, Mr. Thomas, but the young boy's the one I want. I'll be takin' im now."

Billy pushed Robert off the driveway south into some bushes, grabbed Susan with his other arm, his left gimpy one, and pulled her off on the north side at the same time. He picked up a good-sized rock and threw it. The rock didn't hit the man's head as Billy hoped, but it hit his bicep on the arm holding the gun. The pistol pointed down, Billy jumped in front of the mare and yelled, the mare reared, the man slid backwards off the mare, and dropped the gun. Billy took it, pointed it at the man, and then his nerves kicked in. He started to shake.

He tried to hide his shakiness, but felt sure the short guy noticed. He asked Susan to hold the gun on the guy, gave it to her, then sat down and vomited. When he felt better, he hugged Robert, took the gun back, yelled at the mare again to make her run away, and ordered the man to walk toward his mom's barn. He explained to Susan and Robert as they walked. "I'll lock him in the crib in the barn, and then watch to make sure he doesn't get out. Robert, when we get to the house, you go in and explain to Mom why I'm not there. Susan, you walk on home, and if your dad'll come, get him to walk down here and help me decide what to do next."

Robert and Susan both tried to answer at once. Robert won. "I'll go in the house, but I'll be right back out. I don't want you in the barn with this guy by yourself."

Susan waited until Robert finished, then, "I know Dad'll come. And if he won't, I will."

"No, whatever you do, don't you come. I'm already worried about the guy getting in the house where Mom and the boys are. I don't wanna have to worry about you too."

Robert interjected, "Don't worry about it, Billy. After I tell Mom, I'll be right back out, and if the guy tries anything, I'll run'im through with a pitchfork. He better not try anything after I get back."

"You can come back, Robert, but when Susan's dad gets here, you gotta go back in the house to protect Mom."

"I won't. I'm stayin."

They arrived at the driveway, conversations ended, Susan went on around the jog toward her parents' home and Robert went into his mom's house. Billy walked the man to his mom's barn and locked him inside a crib. He stood outside with the pistol and almost immediately, Billy's mom came out to the barn. Billy didn't want to see her. "Get out of here. What if the guy gets out and comes after you? I feared Robert'd come out, but I didn't expect you."

"I won't let Robert out of the house, but he told me everything that happened. I'll go back, but I just want you to know how proud I am that you protected both Robert and Susan. I don't want you to shoot anyone, but if it ever comes to a choice between Robert and a criminal, you know which way to go. I'll go now, but I'll be forever proud of what you did tonight. In the meantime, be careful."

"Thanks, Mom. You better go back to the house now." Her speech delivered, she went.

Billy thought Susan ran most of the way home, because Earl, her dad, came into the barn after only about a half hour. Earl seemed out of breath and looked a little gray, but asked Billy, "Tell me the whole story. Susan told me a little, but I want to hear it all." Earl seemed fine by the end of the account and asked, "Got a rope?"

"Yeah, a hay rope."

"Get it. We'll overpower the guy, tie'is hands behind'is back, tie'is feet together, lock'im back in the crib, and switch off watchin'im all night. I'll watch 'til midnight while you sleep, and then you can watch 'til morning."

"That's all right by me, except I'll sleep out here, not in the house. We got a lot of of extra rope. You think we oughta use it up by wrapping it a few times around his chest and arms?"

"He won't get away, but if 'e did, he's locked in the crib, and if'e got outa there, one of us'd shoot'im. But if you wanna wrap'im, I'll help. As far as where you sleep, that's up to you, but you better get at it, 'cause I'm wakin' you up at midnight."

Billy climbed in a manger and tried to sleep.

Earl woke up when the first light came through the open barn door. He asked, "You got any idee what to do with this guy?"

Billy answered, "No, I hoped you'd know."

"Maybe we oughta take'im down to Jaker and let the sheriff decide."

"Good plan. We can walk him back to my barn, load him in my wagon, and haul him down there. He's not asleep, but I wouldn't mind to wake him up even if he was. You ready now?"

"Yep."

They untied his feet, walked him back to Billy's house, re-tied his feet, and loaded him into Billy's wagon. They hauled him to the sheriff's office in Jaker. They arrived barely before noon, but the sheriff had gone to lunch, so they waited until after one.

The sheriff came back to his office, looked at the three men, and asked Earl, "What's the deal here?"

Even though the sheriff asked Earl, Billy explained, but Mr. Kovachovich finished up. "The guy came after Billy's brother, but I don't doubt my daughter'd o' been hurt too, if Billy hadn't been there. You need to hang a medal on this young fella'."

The sheriff addressed his next question to the tied-up guy. "What's your name?" When the man didn't answer, the sheriff asked, "These men tell the story right?" He still didn't answer, but merely glared at everybody. The sheriff muttered, "I'll look at all my 'wanted' pichers, and see if the guy's wanted anyplace."

The sheriff looked through a tall stack of papers, eventually held one up, and said, "This here one's it. Your name's Mortimer Callagher. You and somebody named Zachariah Smith're wanted in three states for robbery and kidnapping, but my information says Smith's already in custody up in Riverbeach. How'd you get away when they got him?" Still no answer.

"Well, if you ain't talkin', I'll untie you, put you in a cell, and notify the state people." The sheriff looked for weapons, found a pocketknife but nothing else, took off the rope, gave it to Earl, and locked the guy in a cell.

Earl held the rope out toward Billy and said, "This is your rope. We better start back or we won't make it by dark. We passed a grocery store on the way in. We can stop there a minute and buy a bite to eat, but then we need to get back on the road."

After they ate, Earl speculated, "I think we can get back before dark. Can your horses walk a little faster?"

"I don't think so. If I try to speed them up, they'll trot."

"Well, all right. The road's a little rough for a trot, and they'd never last all the way at a trot anyhow."

They talked more, and Billy drove past his farm at dusk, on the way to the Kovachovich home. Susan ran out when she heard the wagon, hugged her dad, then Billy, and called them both heroes. Earl told about the day, and Billy responded to Susan, "We might be heroes, but I'm an awful shaky one. I'd like to stick around and polish up that hero idea, but I don't think I can do it. I'm shot, shaky, worried the guy might be back, and need to get to mom's house for supper and a night's sleep. I hope you don't mind."

Susan nodded. "I'd like to be the one to cook your supper and rock you to sleep, but my time's coming, and I do understand. I'm just glad you got that guy out of here. You're still my hero even if you are shaky and tired."

Billy went to his mom's house and she lit into him the instant he came through the door. "Where have you been all day? Robert and I looked in the barn and found nobody there. Where'd you go?"

Billy hung his head. "I should have come in to tell you. Me and Earl took the tied-up guy to Jaker. The sheriff down there said he's somehow hooked up with the guy that burned your house, and I know he is. He's one of the two I saw leave my barn a while back. He's in jail down there—I hope he never gets loose."

He didn't know if Susan would come to 'their' house the next day on Saturday, so he didn't ask Robert to be there. Susan did come, but he didn't get much work done except to make a stick horse, not because of Robert's absence but because of Susan's presence; each time he thought about work, he decided to kiss Susan first, and then he often forgot about the work part. After two more good meals from a basket, he began to walk Susan home, but they made slow progress because they stopped to talk and kiss often. Susan talked about the wedding during one episode, but Billy wanted to talk about *after* the wedding. Susan spoke first. "We need to decide every detail, so I can pass on the information to my bridesmaids and you can tell your groomsmen."

Billy made a grin he hoped didn't betray his impatience with the wedding talk, but the grin didn't need to do it. His words did. "I could care less about any of that. Should we go into Fiskur on our wedding night, or stay at the farm?"

"Stay at the farm, you Doofus!" Susan's grin seemed genuine. "But first we have to marry. Don't you want to talk about the wedding?"

"I don't wanta talk. I wanta kiss—come back here! I got you now—now you have to kiss me twice!"

They didn't reach Susan's home until after eight o'clock, and ran into a mild lecture from Susan's mom. "I worried about you two. I tried to get Earl to check on you, but he wouldn't go. He just said Billy wouldn't let anything happen to Susan, and that because you're kids, you had things to talk about." Earl grinned.

Both the Thomases and the Kovachoviches went to church on Sunday morning, May 7. Neither Susan nor Billy learned much from the sermon that morning, because they intended to marry at two o'clock that afternoon.

After dinner that day, Billy put on one of the new shirts Susan made, the new pants she made, and wanted to go back to the church with no more delay. Janet persuaded him to hold off until at least one o'clock to begin the walk.

Both Susan and Billy arrived at the church early, but had to wait until the announced starting time of two o'clock, for church and family members to arrive. Pastor Javier told them their wedding would be only his second, but when the time came it went without a hitch, and ended before 2:30. They had to stand around another half hour to shake hands and drink punch, but started for their own home about three. They walked under an overcast sky, but no rain fell until about seven that evening.

They didn't talk as late as they normally did, and Billy apologized. "I didn't get springs under the bed yet. That might bother you, but it won't bother me."

"Me either. We probably won't even notice for at least a week."

32

"Well, I got work to do. I won't be able to stay in it for a whole week!"

Susan's beautiful skin blushed a bright red. "You know what I mean, Billy."

Billy awakened early on Monday after his wedding, noted that rain still fell, frowned, looked at Susan sleeping under his protective arm, smiled, and went back to sleep. They arose late, talked a lot at breakfast but actually said little, and the rain stopped about seven. Billy went outside to feed the animals, including the chickens in his mom's barn. While at his mom's farm, he saw Ben Wilson ride in on a muddy horse. Ben talked to Billy. "I'uz in Riverbeach Saturday night, and saw the sheriff on the street. He told me Zach Smith's boy, Arch, wuz raisin' cain in town earlier, and said he'd spring his dad out of jail. I don't know if that matters to you, but I thought you might wanna know."

"I hope it doesn't matter to me, Mr. Wilson, but it might. I'm obliged to you for telling me."

Ben rode away, back north toward his farm; Billy told his mom about the visit, then went home and told Susan. He told both he'd watch for Zach and Mort as well as he could, and for Arch as well, but they should watch too. He said more to Susan. "I for sure don't want the Arch guy around you. I want to protect you, and will start to carry my rifle again, everywhere I go."

Susan looked doubtful. "Billy, you don't even scare me. How do you expect to scare the Art guy, or Arch, or whatever his name is?"

Billy blustered. "I don't plan to scare him. I plan to put a bullet in him if he comes around here."

"And why would he come around here if his goal is to break his father out of jail?"

"I don't really expect him to show up, but gotta consider he might. It's a little early to plant corn. I intended to work the ground at Mom's today, and here tomorrow, but with all this rain, it's too muddy. I think I'll just take the rifle and walk about halfway between our house and Mom's, and watch for Zach or Mort or Arch."

"Whatever you think, but be really careful."

"I will."

Billy took time off for dinner, chores, and supper, but went back to watch after each. He saw nothing suspicious that day, but waited in the same spot again the next, because the fields remained muddy. He didn't see anything before noon, took time off for dinner again, and saw a rider from the north approach his mom's house in the early afternoon. His brothers were in school and that made him glad, but he worried about his mom. He ran to the house and approached the rider with rifle pointed. The rider turned out to be Ben Wilson again; he raised his hands, allowed a nervous grin to cross his face, and after Billy lowered the rifle, reported he had happy news. "Arch stormed the jail this mornin'. Sheriff Wingate shot at'im and winged'im. Then 'e made the guy promise to leave the state. So I'm thinkin' we're in the clear there."

"Maybe we are. I sure hope we are. Thanks again, Mr. Wilson, for keeping me up to date. I been real worried about my scattered out family."

"Scattered out family?"

"Yeah, my mom and brothers here, and my wife down the road a bit." He pointed.

Billy went inside and told his mom what Ben said, then went home and told Susan. He stopped watching but kept his rifle close, and thought he'd try to work the ground at his mom's place tomorrow.

The sky dumped on them again that night, so the next day, Wednesday, Billy went back to work on furniture in his house. He looked for springs in his junk pile behind the barn, found none, so removed the boards under the bed and replaced them with close-to-gether ropes. He started to make a pie safe with left over lumber from his mom's house, but heard a horse approach from the south in late afternoon. He ran out with his rifle in hand and saw a stranger, an old man bent forward in his saddle. He ordered him to turn back. The stranger said, "My wife's turrible sick, and I'm a' goin' to Fiskur to fetch

34

Dr. Chisholm. I ain't a turnin' back. Shoot me if you must, but I ain't a turnin' back."

"Where you live?"

"Bye." The stranger kicked his horse and went up the road north. Billy ran out in the middle of the road and watched until the man started the jog at his mom's house.

When Billy went back in the house Susan asked, "What was that all about?"

"Maybe I'm a little jumpy. The guy claimed to be going to Fiskur for Dr. Chisholm, and I think he told the truth."

"You're more than a *little* jumpy. You need to relax."

"If it was just me, maybe I'd relax. But I've had mom to worry about since Dad died, and now you too."

Susan kissed him. "I know, Billy, and I understand. Just don't shoot anybody by mistake!"

"All right. I'll make sure to ask plenty of questions before I shoot."

"Not *before. Instead* of."

Billy grinned. "Whatever you say, Dear."

"I have supper nearly ready. Why don't you sit on the bed a few minutes, and I'll bring food to you."

Billy sat, enjoyed his supper, and did no more work that Wednesday. The next day, because the fields remained a muddy mess, he finished the pie safe and a second chair for his house. Susan admired the workmanship, and kissed him some more. He walked on his fields Friday, and didn't really expect to be able to work Saturday, but he hoped. The fields remained heavy Saturday morning, so he decided to use the remaining primer on his mom's house. He noticed a movement in the trees across the road northwest of his mom's house about midmorning, grabbed his rifle, and ran to the spot. He flushed a rabbit out of a brush pile, but nothing else. He knew he needed more paint, so stopped, went home and talked to Susan for a while, then after lunch, went to Fiskur to get the paint. He returned early, began work again, and finished the primer coat that day. Monday forced a decision on him. He could paint more, or work the fields. He judged the fall-plowed dirt perfect to work, and didn't know when it might rain again, so he ran his harrow over the fields. He could plant on Tuesday if more rain didn't come. It didn't, so he planted corn into perfect conditions in both fields, and planned to paint more on Wednesday. But a knock on his door late Tuesday night changed his plan.

CHAPTER FIVE

Another Bad Guy

May 1899

BILLY OPENED THE DOOR and saw his brother, Robert. "Hey, Bud. You look mighty sober tonight."

Robert talked fast and seemed out of breath. "Billy, a guy busted into our house over an hour ago. He's got Mama, Ed and Timmy in there. I got away, but the guy's still there. You gotta come."

"My rifle's right here. You stay with Susan and I'll go right now."

"Billy, I ain't stayin'. I'm goin'."

Susan jumped up and grabbed Billy by the neck. "Billy, maybe you should get help instead. The man might have a gun."

Robert nodded. "He does."

Billy shook Susan off. "I gotta go. Robert, you stay here."

"I ain't stayin."

"Well, I don't have time to argue, but if you go, keep up, and stay outa' my way."

"All right, Billy, but I'm goin'."

Billy grabbed his rifle, ran out the door, and ran north. He showed no caution, but jerked the door open to his mom's new house, burst into the kitchen, and slammed the door when he arrived. A man he didn't know pointed a gun at him before he could raise his rifle. His mom and brothers sat in a corner, white faced and shaking. Billy edged toward them, but soon the door opened, Robert came in and distracted the man for only a short time but long enough for Billy to knock the man's gun down with his rifle barrel. The man didn't drop the gun, but his grip loosened, and Billy stuck the rifle against his chest. He said, "Drop the pistol."

"You think I'm crazy?"

"If you got a lick o' sense, you'll drop it."

A short standoff followed then the man dropped the gun. Billy noted the man had a sling on his left arm, and a cane on the kitchen table. He said, "Real smart of you. Now turn around. Robert, go out to the barn. Get the big hayfork rope back down out of the loft and bring it in here. It's not over the pulleys, but just coiled up on the floor. Mom, pick up the guy's pistol and put it on the table, on the far side away from him."

Robert went back out, Janet put the gun on the table, and Billy began to shake, but held the rifle pointed more or less at the man. Robert came back in with the rope, and Billy sent him on another errand. "Now go back out, go to my house and tell Susan we're all right." Robert went, and Billy approached Arch, the captured man's presumed name, with the rifle in his right hand and the rope in his left.

Arch looked over his shoulder and said, "Let's go outside. I plan to shoot you, and I don't want these kids to see it."

Billy grinned. "How you going to shoot me with your gun on the table? If you want me to tie you outside, that's as good as inside, though. If you want outside, let's go."

"Can I pick up my cane first?"

"Sure, pick up your cane, pick your nose, or pick a peck of flowers, for all I care. Just don't let it slow you down."

"I'm right behind you."

"No, I'll go out behind you. Now move."

The man shook his head, grabbed the cane, raised his right hand with cane in it, and went out the door. Billy intended to tell him to head for the barn, but before he did, the guy asked, "Where we goin'?"

"Out in front of the barn. You walk that far, then I'll tie you and you can sleep in the barn tonight. I'll haul you to Riverbeach to have a chat with the sheriff tomorrow."

The guy whirled around before they got to the barn, pointed a gun at Billy with his left hand, knocked the rifle aside with his right, and said, "What a dummy. Didn't it ever occur to you I might hide another gun in my sling? We'll start walkin' to my farm over in Celyne County now. I'll walk behind, and don't walk too fast, 'cause my left leg's short."

Billy's mind raced, and he tried to stall. "Let me go back in and tell my mom where I'm going."

"Now you act like you think *I'm* the dummy. If you tell anybody where you're goin', they'll send people after you, and I'll have to shoot 'em. Take off and walk, through the woods, not on the road."

"Where are we going?"

"To my farm south of Humphrey. You're gonna be my slave there."

"For how long?"

"'Til I shoot you."

Billy worried. Would he be able to escape and get back home soon, and if not, how would Susan and his mom and brothers make it? If he didn't get back soon would Susan wait for him? He hoped she would, but couldn't know for sure.

"My brother went to tell my wife I'm—what happened. Her dad'll come after you and beat you like a drum if he finds you and me together."

"Shut up and walk."

"You're the boss for now, but you're in big trouble."

The man didn't answer.

They walked east all night alongside the road, and Billy didn't think they made much progress. Indeed, he tried to walk through difficult thickets and mud holes as much as he could and to leave as many tracks and signs as he could. The man commented about it. "You ain't a fast walker, are ya Boy? We had to walk past daylight to get a good start."

They holed up all day in an old chicken house, walked off the road another night, and then the guy allowed Billy to lie around another day. He tried to catch the man asleep, but he seemed super-human. The next night, they walked north on a road, then turned east off it, up a hill and down the other side. They arrived late in the night at a concrete structure with a solid iron door standing open, and with barred windows. The man had been silent all night, but now he said, "Go in th' door. I'll unlock it when mornin' comes, and tell you what to do next."

Billy asked, "How often do you unlock this door?

"That's for me to think about, not you."

"Do you ever forget to lock it back?"

"You think old Arch is as dumb as you? If it ever happens, you act like you don't know. It'll be a test—you stick yore head out and I'll blow it off."

Billy wondered how much time might pass before he escaped. He did intend to escape, but didn't know if he'd do it tomorrow or if he'd need a week or more.

He didn't have a light, but found a flat floor to sleep on, and tried to remember the door location relative to the windows. The windows had no glass, the breeze felt good, and Billy didn't worry about a cold winter wind, because he planned to escape soon. He did worry about Susan, but eventually fell asleep.

Arch didn't come inside the building in the morning, but banged on the door. He yelled, "You git yourself in front o' this'ere door. When I open it, I'll have a gun on you, and you come on out. I'll tell you your first job after you're out." He didn't talk for a moment, but continued to bang, then yelled again, "You there yet?"

"I'm here."

Billy heard the lock turn and saw the door open. He went out into the dark. Arch held up a lantern and hit him in the face with his cane three times. Then he hit his droopy shoulder three times and said, "There's ten cows in th' barn over there. Milk' em." He pointed northeast with his cane, toward a barn.

Billy spit out a tooth and walked toward the barn, but Arch yelled, "I never want to see you walk. Run." Billy, conscious of the gun Arch had, broke into a slow jog. He went in the barn and found it darker in there than outside, but bumped into a bucket and then a cow. She wouldn't stand for him. He suspected the barn might contain a stanchion somewhere, but he found a rope before he found a stanchion, looped the rope over her horns, tied her to a post, and started to milk Arch appeared in a barn door and asked, "Done yet?"

"I'm about half done with the first cow."

"What'cha been doin'? Step it up, we ain't got all day."

Billy stopped with that cow, found another, and almost finished before Arch yelled again. Billy stopped, began to milk a third, and when Arch yelled again, yelled back, "I'm done."

Arch answered, "You better be. I'll check." He held up his lantern, saw an unmilked cow, set the lantern down, came inside, and whacked Billy three times in the face and three times on his bad shoulder with his cane. He ordered him to finish the job and to get on it, and backed out of the barn, all without lowering the gun. Arch didn't bother him again until he finished, even though he had to hunt for a place to empty the bucket. He found a tub with a chicken nest in it, dumped the nest out, and poured milk into the tub. He put the milk in the tub to get rid of it, and to go along with his goal to be insolent and unhelpful.

He looked at the barn door after he found and milked ten cows, to find a trace of daylight and Arch with his gun trained on him. Arch asked, "Ya' gonna' jist leave them cows in th' barn all day?"

Billy then asked, "What do you want me to do with them?"

Arch hit him six more times with the cane and said, "You're the slave, and I'm the owner. One thing you don't do is backtalk me."

Billy spit out another tooth and asked again, "You just want me to put them out in the lot here?"

Arch swung the cane *another* six times and said, "I've a good mind to shoot you now, before you do anything else dumb."

Billy thought, were it not for his family, maybe he'd welcome death at Arch's hand. But he didn't invite it; instead he went back in the barn, drove the cows out, and thought about the best way to rush Arch. He decided to wait, because Arch continued to hold a gun on him. Arch had another question. "What'd you do with the milk?"

Billy jerked a thumb in the direction of the barn. Arch asked, "It's in there?"

"Yep."

"Well bring it out, you blockhead."

"I might spill it."

"If you do, it'll be th' last thing you do."

Billy knew he couldn't carry the full tub out of the barn, so he went back in and dragged the tub out into the lot. Arch said, "You put milk in that filthy tub? A chicken was settin' on eggs in there."

"Yep. The hen flew when I poured milk on her."

"I ain't a' drinkin' it. That milk'll be yours to drink 'til it's gone. Next time use your head, if you still have one by then." He used the cane six more times on Billy.

Arch continued to bully Billy for a while, pointed to a pasture to put the cows in, then said, "There's two horses in the barn. Harness 'em." Billy could see in the barn now that the sun had risen to the horizon. He found the horses and harnessed them. While looking for the horses, he noticed a barrel with a cover, and supposed maybe that's where milk should go.

Arch gave obscure directions and hit Billy with the cane several more times, but eventually told him to hook up to the planter, and plant into worked dirt behind the 'cell,' as Billy thought of it. He intended to escape when he came to the far end of the field, but saw Arch with a rifle trained on him. His spirits sank as he realized Arch would never let him out of his gun sights.

He planted the field, put the planter back where he found it, unharnessed the horses, and put them in the same pasture with the cows. He went after the cows and milked them in the dark again. Arch allowed him no break, no food, or no drink, until he finished, then said "If you wanna drink from the tub, go ahead. That's all I got for ya'." Billy drank like a horse, appreciated the dirty milk, and almost felt glad to be locked in his 'cell.' He felt for a bare spot on the floor and slept soundly until awakened the next day when Arch banged on the door again.

He worked for Arch all summer and beyond, until he lost track of the summers. He never found a decent opportunity to escape, and thought he might someday freeze to death in the 'cell,' under a pile of blown-in snow. Arch didn't allow time off, ever, not even a bathroom break. Billy had to deposit his wastes either on the 'cell' floor, or in his overalls. Besides that, Arch's cane had knocked out all Billy's front and side teeth and scarred his face and body. He thought often of his family, remembered he'd never gone to the courthouse with Susan to put her name on the deed to the farm, and realized he must somehow get back to Susan, his mom, and his brothers. One summer day, although he knew every conversation with Arch ended with cane contact, he spoke to Arch. "You know, Arch, you're as much my slave as I am yours."

Arch worked him over good with the cane, then asked, "How you figger?"

"You won't let me leave here, but you can't leave here either, because you know I'll be gone when you came back, and a lawman'd soon be in here looking for you."

"Don't you worry your bloody head about that none. I got ever'thing I need right here. I got a farm, a garden, cows, chickens, and a dumb slave. An' if I do wanna git sompin out, I make you leave it out by the road and a messenger takes care of it from there. What else I need?"

Billy turned his back when he saw the cane coming again, but when Arch had him plow a field that fall, he purposefully steered the plow into a rock, and broke the share. He first taunted Arch. "Look at that, Arch, a busted share. You gonna go to town and get another one? Ain't it awful!"

Arch beat him with the cane worse than he ever had before. He realized Arch didn't care if he lived or died. "Please, Arch, go get another one. I won't run away. Please."

Arch gave him a couple more shots with the cane, and said, "Git yore sorry carcass up outta the dirt and put them share pieces on the flat rock out by the road. I'll wait in the trees with my rifle on ya. You'd better not try anything if you wanna live."

Billy took the share to the road, and even tried to run when Arch ordered him to, but he couldn't. Arch noted his inability, and screamed, "Yore about wore out. I'll have to shoot ya afore year-end."

Billy opened his mouth to answer, but quickly closed it again. That night in his 'cell,' he decided to try to bluff Arch, and if it worked, great. If not, then he'd be dead, but that'd be better than to die later as Arch's slave. He waited until Arch had him plow the field south of the 'cell,' then waited more, for a rain. Arch banged on the door as usual the morning after the next rain. Billy yelled in response, "I'm not coming out. You'll have to come in and get me."

"I ain't comin' in."

"Then I'll stay here all day. Maybe you ought to consider milking the cows yourself, while I sleep some more."

"You ornery ingrate. I'll come in and beat you to a pulp."

Billy stood close to the wall just inside the door. When Arch came in, Billy pushed him from behind, and they wrestled for the gun. It discharged a couple times without hitting anybody, then Billy got it and meant to throw it out a window, but it bounced off a bar and fell in front of Arch. Arch picked it up and shot at Billy, but got only one shot at first, because Billy ran out the open door and around behind the concrete building. He didn't slow, but sprinted south in the mud across the long field, and hoped to jump in the gulley he'd seen at the far side. He thought he could run faster in the sticky mud than Arch could with his game leg, but he knew Arch could move along at a decent clip when he wanted to. He heard Arch order him to stop, but still didn't slow. He heard a bullet go by just as he jumped into the gulley. He turned up the gulley as he planned, and hoped Arch would turn down it. He already knew the trees thinned at the upper end and thickened at the lower; he meant Arch to miss his upward turn, and to expect Billy to turn the other way.

Arch didn't fall for Billy's ploy, but took a moment to find tracks, and followed. Billy saw him, ran flat out, all the way out the end of the gully, then briefly toward the concrete building, and turned back beside the gully. When he thought Arch should be farther up than his position, he ran back to the gulley, jumped in again, and came face to face with Arch holding his gun. Arch grinned. "Will you never learn, Boy? You cain't outsmart old Arch."

Billy slowed a second, didn't respond to Arch, but picked up speed again and ran full blast into him. He tried to knock the gun away as he went. He only partly succeeded and took another bullet in his left shoulder, but left Arch flat on his back in the bottom of the gulley. He ran down-gulley a few seconds, then climbed out the south side, and ran perpendicularly away from it. He could feel a lot of blood flow from his shoulder down his arm, and knew he couldn't run much longer. He looked for a place to hide as he ran, didn't find one, but came to a road. He went over the fence into the road and ran west up the middle; he thought—and hoped—if Arch followed him, he wouldn't shoot him in a public place. He went up a short hill, started down the other side, saw a woman outside a house off to the left, wobbled, waved, and then fell on his face.

He expected to bleed to death there, and waited for it to happen. He didn't pass out, however, because an old man with a full beard and a felt hat arrived soon, with two horses and a wagon. He didn't look as skinny as Billy, but skinny, and taller. He lacked the middle finger on his right hand and wore the standard overalls and blue shirt common to the area. He loaded Billy into the wagon and took him to the house he'd seen. The woman there sat him in a chair and looked at his shoulder. She got a dishrag and talked to him.

"Hold this where the blood's a comin' out. Maybe it'll stop it." She turned to the man. "Will, you git into Humphrey as fast as you can, and git Dr. Merriwether out here quick . . . Don't stand there, git."

The woman turned back to Billy. "My husband's gone for Dr. Merriwether. They'll be back soon, but let me clean you up and look at that shoulder better. How'd it happen? Whew-ee, you stink, Boy. Ain't you cleaned up lately?"

Billy knew he looked and smelled terrible, because he'd not shaved, bathed, or changed his shirt or overalls for almost three years, but told the woman everything, including his name.

"Your story don't make sense, but it's jist crazy enough I believe it . . . the bleedin's stopped. What'd you do?"

Billy didn't tell her again. He felt as woozy as before, but noticed the woman had no more meat on her bones than the man, stood a good foot shorter, and maybe carried a few less years. She had on men's overalls like the man did, under a severe, almost manly hairdo. She brought a wash pan, water, cloth, and her husband's razor. She used them, then said, "You're nuthin' but skin and bones, and your clothes are tore almost clear off. Your feet's all cut up too. Where's your shoes?" The woman didn't give Billy time to answer, but went on. "Will's clothes'll be a little loose on ya but he's got some clean ones, and he'll help ya put'em on when he comes. When he takes Dr. Merriwether back to Humphrey, he'll stop and talk to Sheriff Johnson. Ever'body always thought somethin' bad went on at the Arch Smith place, but nobody ever knew what it was. My name's Edith and my husband's name's Will Hastings."

Billy seized on the "somethin' bad" comment, drew back in his chair, and begged, "Please don't send me back there. I need to get home and check on my family."

Edith responded, "I won't send ya nowhere. The sheriff'll decide that, but he might want ya to stick around as a witness. If he does that, ya can stay here, of course."

Billy set his jaw and said, "I gotta go home *now*."

Edith shook her head. "You're in no shape to travel today, and won't be tomorrow. Maybe ya can set in a wagon the next day, Saturday. Will can take ya home then, if ya eat good. Where'd you say you live? Do you know what day it is?"

"I live over at the north edge of Joaquin County, and I can wait until Saturday to go there, but not a day longer. I'd love to eat every day, but I don't have any money. And I don't know what day, month, or year it is."

"Ya don't need money, Boy. Ya can eat and stay here, with Will and me. And ya can start with breakfast. Will and me wuz about to set down when I seen ya in the road. Do ya think ya can make it to the kitchen table? This is April 23, Wednesday, 1902."

"Sure, I can make it. Wow! Old Arch had me locked up for close to three years." Billy staggered and almost passed out on the way to the kitchen, but Edith had a platter of fried eggs, another of fried bacon, a pan of biscuits, and a bowl of gravy on the table. "That's beautiful, Ma'am. I'll try to hold back, but I want it all!"

He ate a small amount, and apologized. "Edith, that food is the best I ever tasted, and is the only for a long time, but I just can't eat more."

Will returned after a short time, with Dr. Merriwether. The doctor didn't do much, except to look at Billy and to make a couple comments. "The boy didn't break any bones or damage any vital organs, but he's lost a lotta' blood. Don't let this young fella' do much and get clean clothes on him . . . make sure he eats good for a few weeks, and he'll be all right."

Edith answered. "That's been our plan all along, Doc. I want Billy here to tell you what's goin' on at the Arch Smith place, and if Will don't beat you to it, to git Sheriff Johnson out here to check it all out."

Billy told his story again, and ended with "And I won't stay for a trial. I need to go on home and check on my family."

Dr. Merriwether smiled. "The sheriff will decide about that part."

"That's fine if the sheriff decides right, but if he wants me to stay, I won't."

Edith patted him one time on his left shoulder, caused him to wince, and she stopped in mid-pat before a second one hit. "It'll all work out, Billy. Will and the sheriff'll be back here directly, and if I see Arch a comin' down the road afore they git here, he'll get a load o' buckshot in the face." She took a shotgun off hooks above the door, and laid it on the kitchen table.

Will returned by noon, and Sheriff Johnson showed up in mid-afternoon; Billy had to tell his story one more time. The sheriff wore a pistol at his belt, flashed bulging muscles, and slightly intimidated Billy. The sheriff asked, "What's your name, Boy?"

"Billy Thomas."

"Well, I don't mind tellin' you, Billy, that tale's hard to believe. This concrete buildin' you talk about—why didn't anybody ever see it?"

Billy shook his head. "I thought it was there. Maybe I was wrong."

Sheriff Johnson's face flushed red. "You say you lived in it three years. You *know* whether it's there—is it, or isn't it?"

A weak smile crossed Billy's face. "It's there."

"So why didn't anybody ever see it?"

"You ever go by the Arch Smith place and see a hill out front? It's under the hill, Sheriff. I don't care if you believe me or not, but it's there."

Edith frowned, glared at both Billy and the sheriff, and said, "Ya go look, Dan. We all know Arch's up to somethin', so ya go look. Be careful, but go look. I believe the boy; if he's lyin', how'd he get so skinny? How'd he lose all them teeth? How'd he git shot? How'd he git all them whiskers that I can go out to the trash pile and show ya if ya wanna see'em? How'd his overalls get so tore up? I can show ya those too if you wanna look."

Sheriff Johnson averted his eyes. "Oh, I'll go look, but I still can't believe Billy's story."

Edith replied, "Nobody cares if ya believe it, so long as you check it out. Don't tell nobody where you found Billy, or Will, me, and

Billy'll *all* be in danger."

Edith and the sheriff argued more, the sheriff eventually agreed again to stop at the Smith place on his way back to Humphrey, and Billy noticed a raging hunger again. He didn't eat much, but also didn't miss any meals until Saturday, when Will took him toward home. Even then, Edith put sandwiches in a lunch box for them, along with milk in two separate bottles.

CHAPTER SIX

Billy Goes Home

April 1902

BILLY'S EXCITEMENT GREW as Will took him ever closer to his home. His apprehension grew too, because he didn't know what reception he'd receive. When Will passed his mom's house, he suspected a problem, because he saw a goat in the yard.

"Uh-oh, Will. I saw a goat, and Mom always claimed to hate goats. Do you suppose she's moved away?" He also privately wondered if Zach or Mort had returned.

"Don't borrow no trouble, Son. Why would she move?"

Billy didn't answer, but tried to look ahead to see his house. When Will stopped in his driveway, and he saw the weeds in the yard and garden, the condition of the barn roof, and the bare curtainless windows in the house, he almost knew. "I got a sick feeling, Will, there's nobody here. I'll look."

He left the wagon and beat on the door, but when no one answered, both his shoulders slumped, the good and the bad, and he walked back to the wagon. He tried to put on a good face for Will, and reported, "Nobody's here. Maybe my wife went up the road to live with my mom. Let's go back to the last house we passed."

Billy went to the door of the house he thought belonged to his mom, closed his mouth so she wouldn't see the gaps where his teeth should be, and knocked. He stood speechless for a moment when a

51

woman he didn't know opened the door. She waited a few seconds, and said, "Yes?"

Billy forgot about his missing teeth. "I'm looking for Janet Thomas. Does she live here?"

"My husband and I bought this house and farm at auction. I think the seller's name might have been Thomas."

"Do you know where she is?"

"No."

Billy went back to the wagon, and asked, "Can you take me one more place? North about two miles?"

"Sure, Son."

They went to the Kovachovich place. Billy first thought it looked vacant too, but walked around back and found a man there, not Earl. He asked, "Who are you?" He tried to talk with a mostly closed mouth.

The man answered, "Ted Dickinson. My dad owns a bank down in Joaquin County, and foreclosed on this place after the Kovachoviches died. He sent me up here to check on it."

"Are both Earl and Mary Kovachovich dead?"

"Yes."

"Do you know what happened to their daughter, Susan?"

"Sure. She took care of her parents as long as they lived, then married old man Little. I don't know where he lives, but they say he's rich. They say he got that way when he was just a pup; he married a rich old widder. She up and died, and that's where Little's money came from."

Billy sat down on a stump behind the house and cried. His great violent sobs tore at his sore shoulder, but he couldn't stop. Ted looked uncomfortable and walked around the corner of the house. Billy cried for a few minutes, regained control, then went around front, where Will and Ted waited. "You might as well go on back, Will. There's nothing here for either of us."

"You sure, Billy?"

"That's what I said, Will. Go on home." Billy's voice had a bitter edge he quickly regretted, but Will already had the horses turning back toward the tee to the east.

Billy stood and thought a long minute. Then he stepped into the road and turned south. He walked all the way past his house, and up the long driveway to Ron and Gertrude Knight's place. He knocked on the door, and 'Gertie' answered. Her face broke into a wide smile, and she shouted, "Ron's gonna be glad to see you. He's at the barn now, but should be back real quick. Come on in here. I want to look at you. How are you?"

He opened his mouth, then grinned, and said, "I'm fine except for some teeth out."

"You sure are skinny. If you were a fattening hog, I'd let the wolves have you!"

Billy went in and made small talk until Ron arrived. Then he went right to his question. "Do you know where Susan is?"

He directed the question to Ron, but Gertie answered. "She didn't stay even one night at your place after you ran off, but went up and took care of her folks until they both died, then real quick, maybe a week, or two at most, she married the Little guy from somewhere around Riverbeach."

"When'd that happen?"

"About a year and a half back."

Billy'd heard this same story already. It confirmed that he'd lost Susan, and he almost cried again, but held it to watery eyes this time. And this time he looked at Gertie when he asked, "You know what happened to Mom?"

Mrs. Knight shook her head no. "A month or more before Susan's wedding she had a farm auction. She had three days to get out, but stayed only one. It seemed like the earth opened and swallowed her up. Nobody knows where she went, why, or how she got there."

Ron added, with an accusing tone in his voice, "Arter you run off, the spirit seemed ta go out o' 'er. I tried ta help'er, but she didn't seem ta care 'bout nuthin' no more."

Billy decided to find his mom before he came back to see if he still had a farm, and before he tried to knock down the notion he ran away. "Well, thanks. I gotta go now and try to find Mom."

Gertie frowned and said, "Not tonight. Ron's already done his evening chores; you stay for supper and talk. Wait 'til after breakfast in the morning to go anywhere."

The idea of talk seemed all right, but supper and breakfast especially appealed to Billy. He still thought he could eat a ton, and still wanted to, so he agreed to stay. But he formed a little plan during the night, left the Knight's soon after breakfast, and walked into the telegraph office in Fiskur, forgetting it would be closed on Sunday. He waited overnight behind a straw stack outside of town, and went back on Monday, When there, he went back to the telegraph office and spoke to the telegraph operator, a middle-aged man with a name tag that identified him as Samuel A. Mesker. He told Samuel the entire story about losing his mom, said he wanted to find her, and added, "She once had a sister somewhere back east, maybe Indiana or Ohio. She called her Kitty. I don't know her last name. Can you find her?"

Sam shook his head and answered, "You sound like you've not been around the block many times, Son. If you want to give me a specific message, to a person in a specific place, I can send a telegram. But I can't go searching around for somebody with no name and no address."

Billy turned to walk away, but Samuel called after him, "Maybe you can buy a bunch of postcards and mail them to churches in those states. Some'll no doubt go in a trash can, but some might get passed around, and you might hit pay dirt somewhere."

He had no better idea. "You got a dollar I can borrow? I don't know when I can pay it back, but you can be sure I will, someday."

Samuel shook his head. "I have one, but not for lending."

Billy headed for the Ben Wilson farm. As he went, he stopped at a farm with both a big house and a big barn. He knocked at the house, and an older but still attractive woman in a nice dress, but no shoes, answered the door. He asked, "You need farm help?"

The woman partly closed the door. "No."

"I'm a good worker, Ma'am."

"My husband doesn't employ fighters with scarred faces and no teeth." She closed the door all the way.

Billy continued his walk to the Ben Wilson farm. He knocked on the door there, and a woman who turned out to be Mrs. Wilson, Sally, came to the door. Ben had a not-yet-old, tall lean look, but the woman at the door looked older, shorter, and fatter than Ben. He asked for Ben, and then tried to limit himself to only one subject when Ben arrived, but Ben pried out his entire story before Billy could inquire, "Can I work for you and sleep in your barn until I earn a dollar? I want to buy some postcards, and I have experience at going many days without food."

Ben smiled. "Of course. Our busy season is here already, and I'll offer you room and board—in the house, not in the barn—plus a dollar a week for as long as you want to stay."

Billy forgot about his bad shoulder and jumped high in the air. Then he used his good arm to shake Ben's hand. He said, "I accept. You won't be sorry, because I'll be the best worker you ever had. Can I start this afternoon?"

"Sure, after you eat lunch." Ben grinned. "Are you sure you can eat? I don't see any teeth—Sally didn't expect company, so you won't get a lot, but you'll get as much as anyone else does."

Billy grinned too. "I have teeth, they're just hard to see." He opened his mouth, and pointed to a few remaining back teeth. He briefly wondered if he should warn Ben about Arch or Zach or Mort, but then decided they'd never find him there.

Billy worked the remainder of the week, and insisted he work until noon on Saturday as well, to make up for his late start on Monday. Back on the first Monday evening, he went to see Pastor Tom Buller at a Methodist church in Riverbeach, and asked for the names and addresses of all Methodist churches in Indiana and Ohio. He explained why he wanted them and why he picked that denomination

(He thought maybe there'd be more Methodist churches than others in Indiana and Ohio). Pastor Buller said he wanted to help, but might need a few days to find all the information, and suggested Billy return on Thursday evening. He did, and the pastor had a long list for him. Saturday afternoon, Billy borrowed a pencil from Mrs. Wilson, took his dollar, walked to the post office in Riverbeach, and bought a hundred penny postcards. He sat on a bench outside the post office, wrote a hundred times, *I'm Billy Thomas, looking for my mom and brothers, Janet, Robert, Ed, and Timmy Thomas. Will you write back to me if you know where they are?* He addressed all hundred postcards and carefully added his name, C/O Ben Wilson at RR 2, Riverbeach, Missouri. The next Saturday he bought enough post cards to finish the list. He expected a useful answer in a few days, but waited more than three weeks before he received a letter from a Pastor Pettijohn in Grandview, Indiana. Pastor Pettijohn wrote he didn't know Janet Thomas, but a friend, Pastor Argyle in nearby Lewisport, Kentucky told him Janet attended his church.

Billy could hardly stand still. He told the Wilsons. "I found my mom and brothers, somewhere in Kentucky." The Wilsons asked him dozens of questions he couldn't answer. He went back that very evening to tell Pastor Buller, but couldn't find him, so wrote in dust on a window at the front of the church. He wrote, *Thanks. I found them. Billy.*

He walked to the Riverbeach train station Saturday, to learn the cost of a train ticket to Lewisport. He talked to the agent there, who answered, "No train runs to Lewisport, but one goes to Evansville, and you can walk from there. Look at this map of the area." He pulled a folded map out of a drawer, unfolded it, and pointed. "You can walk across the Ohio River on a bridge at Rockport." He pointed again, and told him the cost of a ticket—more money than Billy had. So he decided to ride with hobos on freight cars. He knew where a train headed east near Riverbeach, where it slowed as it climbed a gentle slope, and planned to wait there as soon as he could leave Ben. He walked back to the Wilson farm, explained his plan, then added, "You've been great to me, Ben, and I hate to say this, but I want to—must—go. I'll work a couple more weeks if you want me to."

Ben grinned. "You told me when you started what you were up to, and I'd planned all along to replace you with the boy down the road when you got ready to go. You can go this instant, tomorrow, or whenever you want to. I'm not Arch, after all."

"Thanks, Ben. I don't know if it'll ever matter, but I'll never forget how you've treated me." He walked to his planned location beside the track, and waited for a train. Eventually a train came, he ran to an empty flat car, and climbed on. The train stopped at every little town it went through, and Billy feared he'd be found. He jumped off in a nearby town and hid behind a building labeled Espy Station. The train left, and he climbed on the next one. He knew he needed to change trains in St. Louis, but didn't know which one to take. He figured he got the wrong one when he came to Indianapolis, not Evansville. He cleaned up in a railroad water lake, went into the station as a customer, and asked how to get to Evansville. The agent told him, and told him the cost; he couldn't afford a ticket for even the last part of his trip, so he turned to leave the station. The agent called to him, and suggested a livery stable where he might ask about the cost of a horse rental. Billy went to the stable, and could afford the cost of a horse and saddle for a week, so he rented one. He rode to the bridge at Rockport, across it, and on to Lewisport and to Pastor Argyle's church. Pastor Argyle happened to be at the church that Saturday afternoon in June, and told Billy how to find Janet Thomas on Pell Street. He grinned at the thought that Arch, Zach, nor Mort would never think to look for him in Kentucky.

CHAPTER SEVEN

Billy Meets Janet

June 1902

BILLY WENT TO THE PLACE Pastor Argyle sent him, and on the way he decided to forget about his missing teeth. He knocked on the door of a house, and his anticipation rose sky-high. A man and a woman, each not much older than Billy, came to the door and Billy asked, "May I see Janet Thomas?"

The woman answered, "I'm Janet Thomas, and this is my husband Ryan."

Billy's spirits fell with what he thought might be an audible thud. He hesitated, and the woman asked, "Are you Billy Thomas?"

"Yes, but you're not my mom."

"I know. Pastor Argyle told me you might come; I've only been married about a year, and am not anybody's mom."

Billy ran his hand over his face, swallowed, and hesitated more; the woman continued. "I'm the secretary to George Evans, Superintendent of Schools in Hancock County. He doesn't have a record of every child in school in the US, but he can get it. I'll ask him to find your brothers—Robert, Ed and Timmy—is that what Pastor Argyle told me? He'll probably ask me do it, and I'll stay after work every night until I find them. And when I do, where will you be?"

Billy hadn't considered a question like that. He hesitated a third time, then said, "I rented a horse"— he pointed — "in Indianapolis, and

59

must have him back by Tuesday afternoon. I can look for temporary work there, and check for mail with the livery stable every day. Will you send a letter to me there?"

"Sure . . . but Ryan, can you employ Billy down at your lumber-yard here in Lewisport, while I look?" She directed the question to the young man, Ryan Thomas, her husband.

Billy didn't wait for an answer. "I'd love that if it could happen, but I have to take the horse back."

"Oh, yeah. I forgot that already! So yes, I can send information to you at the livery stable. Do you know the address?"

"Almost. It's owned by Eb Dyer, on Rough Street in Indianapolis."

Ryan said, "I've seen it, but don't know the address. I'll make that my project, to find an address for it."

Janet added, "Don't expect anything real fast. It could take some time to find your brothers. Do you have any thoughts on where they might be?"

"Mom talked about Indiana and Ohio. They might be in one of those states."

"Well, that narrows the territory down a lot. I'll look there first."

"Thanks." Billy walked back toward the street to where he'd tied the horse, climbed on, and headed back to Indianapolis with drag-ging spirits.

Billy came back to Indianapolis on Tuesday, June 17. He re-turned the horse to the livery and explained what he intended to Eb, and why. Eb grinned. Billy thought him about the age and smallish size his dad would be. Eb said, "You can work here as long as you want. I don't like to feed horses and muck out stalls anyway. I can't pay you much more than enough to eat on, but you can sleep in the stable if you're willing."

Billy grinned too, and stuck out his hand. "I'll shake on that, Mr. Dyer. I think that's a great offer, and if you'll show me what to do, I'll start right now."

"It's almost time to feed, so I'll show you that part, and you probably already know how to fork horse manure out back. I'll show you where to put it."

Billy found Eb a good boss in many ways, much better than Arch, but Eb seemed picky about minor details. He criticized Billy every day for one thing or another, or for several others. The third day exemplified his complaints. "Not a terrible job today, Billy, but look at old Ruby there. She's not finished with her oats yet, meaning you fed her too much. And look at old Bob. I can see every one of his ribs. He needs more feed. And look at the straw in the empty stall." He pointed. "It's not as spotless as it oughta' be. You gotta do a better feeding job and clean better."

Billy didn't point out that he fed each horse exactly the amount Eb showed him the first day, that Ruby eats slow, that Bob looked emaciated the first time he saw him, or that the empty stall had been empty since before he came there. Instead, he worried that he might be fired. He didn't get fired, but felt he'd never be able to satisfy Eb. He also started to expect a letter from Lewisport as early as Monday the 19th, but all of June went by and half of July before a letter arrived. It was from Janet, but didn't contain information. She merely asked him to be patient, said she'd searched all through both Indiana and Ohio with no result, and had started on Kentucky, because she could get information about Kentucky faster than she could about other states. Billy hadn't been sure his mom went to either Ohio or Indiana, and didn't have a reason to prefer any other state over Kentucky, so he didn't answer. He made up his mind to stay in Indianapolis indefinitely, and suspected he'd never see his mom again. He waited through July with no more letters, but he received one from Janet Thomas during the first week in August. She said she found Billy's brothers in Strick, in far northeastern Kentucky. After his hopes rose and fell with Janet and Ryan, he tried not to be excited about the letter, and merely wrote a postcard addressed to Janet Thomas, Strick, Kentucky. He wrote on the postcard, *"I'm looking for you. I've come from Sinfe County in Missouri, and if you think I could be your son, please write to me at 312 Rough Street, Indianapolis, Indiana. Billy Thomas.*

Billy mailed the letter on Wednesday, August sixth. Excitement built in him despite a major effort to suppress it, and when Eb gave him a letter from Janet Thomas in Strick, Kentucky on Monday, he opened it on the spot and hoped Eb didn't see his hands shake. The short letter filled his every hope. After the salutation it continued, *'I thought you were gone forever, and almost couldn't bear the loss of you and Steve too. I've already told your brothers, and they're wild with anticipation. How soon can you come?'*

Billy enlisted Eb's help, and found John Chrisman, a man bound for Charleston, West Virgina, by way of Huntington not far from Strick, with two horses and a spring wagon. John planned to stop for him at sunup the next day, and Billy sent a return letter to his mom. *Expect me around the middle of next week, maybe as early as Tuesday the nineteenth.*

John Chrisman didn't show at sunup, and finally in late morning sent word with a neighbor that his wife broke her leg and he wouldn't go to Charleston soon, if ever. Billy tried to handle the news, and did for a few minutes, but as soon as he could get alone in the stable, he cried into the mane of old Bob. When he recovered, he looked for Eb again, and asked him to help find another wagon or buggy east. Eb found another, a buggy, but a couple more days went by, and Billy didn't leave Indianapolis until Friday, August fifteenth, with Bob Jimenez headed for Crockett, probably more than a two-day walk from Strick. He mailed another postcard to his mom. *I've been delayed. I now hope to arrive on the twenty-second or twenty-third. Billy Thomas.* He showed up at her house on 3rd Street on Friday evening the twenty-second, Robert's fourteenth birthday. A light shone through a window of the house, although it was still dusky outside. The house looked small and badly maintained. Billy stood a moment, then walked to the door and knocked. Robert opened the door, yelled, rushed Billy, and jumped up to grip him around the neck. Ed and Timmy followed close behind and grabbed him around the legs. His mom followed and wrapped her arms around his chest. He laughed out loud and exclaimed, "I feel hemmed in, but haven't been this happy since Arch got me!"

CHAPTER EIGHT

Strick/Boston

August 1902 / September 1904

BILLY FELT TIRED AND READY TO SLEEP, but he didn't see even one bed inside when he entered the two-room house. His mom asked, "Who's Arch"

"I don't even want to talk about Arch. Maybe we'll get to him tomorrow. Look at you, Robert—you've grown a foot. And so have you Ed. You've jumped up more than that, Timmy."

Timmy grinned, but asked, "Can you call me Tim now? Nobody in Strick calls me Timmy."

"Yeah, Tim. I'm so glad to see you, I'll call you Bill, or Bart, or . . . Bub, or anything you want!"

Janet said, "Look at me." Billy did, and Janet continued, "You look older, and where are your teeth?"

Billy grinned. "I *am* older. And where my teeth went is part of that long story I hope we can put off until tomorrow."

"You must meet your Aunt Kitty tomorrow, too. She knows you're coming here, and wants to meet you."

Billy asked, "Where's she live?"

"In the big house out back. She inherited our parents' house."

"Oh." Billy didn't much care to meet Kitty, and the news she lived in the "big house" didn't add to his interest. He looked instead at Robert, and asked, "What've you been up to, Bud?"

Robert answered, "I'm about to start back to school, but I've had a job cutting grass for Aunt Kitty this summer. She has about a hundred thousand square feet, and it's all I can do to keep up with it."

Billy asked, "Does Aunt Kitty pay you pretty good?"

"Oh, she doesn't pay in money, but lets us stay in this house. I don't know if that's good or not."

Billy's mom jumped back into the conversation. "I bet Kitty can help you find a job here too, Son."

"Now that Susan's gone, I suppose here's as good as any other place."

"She's not gone, but even if she is, you can't blame her, Son, after you ran off and left her like that."

"I didn't run off, Mom. I was stolen. That's all part of the story I hoped to leave until tomorrow, but we can do it now. You want to hear about it?"

"Of course, Dear, if you want to tell about it." Billy told his mom (and brothers) the entire story about his enslavement by Arch, and even added an account of his efforts to find them.

A look of doubt crossed his mom's face. "Why didn't you tell us what happened, or at least write to us?"

"I couldn't, Mom. Arch didn't give me any money, any time off to go buy postcards, and I had no way to communicate with anybody. He would have killed me if I made a move to do it. I would've if I could've."

Her doubtful look remained. "Well, whatever you say, Son. I'm just glad you're back now."

His brothers exclaimed almost in unison, "So am I!"

Robert added, "I believe you, Billy. I've thought about how I got away the night the Arch guy came. I think he planned for me to escape and for you to come. He could have shot me as I left, and he could have hurt us all, but he didn't. I think he had it all planned out."

Janet looked at Robert and said, "Don't blame yourself, Son. You were young then, and you're still young. You don't know what Arch wanted to do."

Billy responded to Robert and to his mom. "Thanks, Robert, for believing me. And Mom, I didn't run away. I thought about you and worried about you every single day. We can talk to the Hastings' or Sheriff Johnson when we get back, and I'm sure they'll tell you all about Arch Smith."

Janet answered, "Billy, I hope you don't go back, but the boys and I plan to stay here. We have a nice quiet life here, Kitty takes care of us, and it just doesn't make sense to leave."

"Don't you think I'll take care of you, Mom?"

"I know you meant well for a time, but you were too young, and didn't have the judgment or stick-to-itiveness Kitty and I have. You may not have those yet."

Billy shrugged. "Can I sleep here?"

"Of course you can, Son. None of us has a bed, but I make a real good pallet, if I do say so myself!" She grinned.

"Well, I don't know what time it is, but it must be late. I walked all day, I'm tired, and I bet my brothers are tired too."

Janet made four pallets on the floor in one room, another in the kitchen for her, blew out the light, and everybody went to bed. Billy thought a few minutes before he fell asleep. He realized his 'homecoming' wasn't exactly as he expected, and he hoped he could someday persuade his mom he didn't voluntarily run away.

Morning came and Janet cooked breakfast. Billy thought his relationship with his brothers hadn't changed, but his mom seemed more reserved than before. After breakfast, she sent Ed over to Kitty's house to make an appointment for her and the boys, including Billy, to visit. Ed came back and said, "Aunt Kitty's servant said we could come at nine."

Billy asked Ed, "Aunt Kitty has a servant?"

"Yes."

"What's his name?"

"It's a her. I don't know her name and I usually don't talk to her. She just tells me things Aunt Kitty says."

"How old is she?"

"Old. Older'n Mom. Like I said, I usually don't talk to her, but just get instructions from her."

Janet ended the discussion. "Her name's Cindy Lou. She's nice, she's a couple of years older than Kitty, and she's been with Kitty for over thirty years. It's almost time to go."

Janet spiffed up herself and the younger boys, but Billy intentionally mussed up his hair and pulled his handkerchief partly out of his hip pocket. He practiced showing his lack of teeth, and they went for the nine am appointment. A servant (Cindy Lou) met them at the door of the big house, took them inside, seated them, and said she'd find Miss Kitty. They waited a short time and then Kitty Carmichael swept into the room and greeted them. Billy stared. Janet and Kitty looked almost exactly the same, except Kitty had on an expensive dress and Janet a cheap one. Billy's mom introduced him, and Kitty asked him, "What prompted you to come back?"

Billy tried to inject exactly the right amount of sarcasm into his voice. "I wanted to meet you, Miss Kitty."

"My word, Boy, what did the other fella look like?"

"What?"

"The fella that knocked your teeth out."

"He doesn't have a scratch on him. He's tough, Aunt Kitty."

Kitty talked with Janet for a few minutes, then announced she had important things to do and called for Cindy Lou, who ushered the Thomas family outside.

Billy asked, "Mom, do you really like Kitty?"

"I have to, Son. I have to think about your brothers—who else will take care of us if Kitty doesn't?"

Billy wanted to shake his mom, and to yell, 'I will.' Instead, he sighed and walked on ahead.

They reached the smaller Thomas house, and Billy asked, "When do you want to go back to Sinfe County?"

Janet scowled and said, "Why would we want to go back? I sold my farm, the county sold yours for back taxes, and there's nothing there for us. You need to find an honest job here in Strick, and plan to stay."

"Do you think farming's not honest work? Do you think Dad didn't do honest work?"

"No, I didn't mean that."

"You said last night that Susan's not gone. Tell me about that."

"Well, she might be gone. I don't know where she is. When you took off, she went back to live with her parents, the boys and I moved back home, and I suppose she's still with her parents." Billy briefly considered going back to Sinfe County alone, but quickly discarded the idea as unfair to his brothers. He suspected his mom knew something about Susan he didn't, but saw no reason to believe she'd tell him anything about her. And since he knew about Susan's marriage, it probably didn't matter anyway. He supposed he should attend church tomorrow with his family, then look for a job on Monday, and plan to stay in Strick for many years. He didn't feel inclined, however, to accept job-hunting help from his Aunt Kitty. Billy stayed in the house all morning on Saturday with his mom and brothers, but after dinner he asked Tim, "What do you guys usually do on a Saturday afternoon?"

"We throw a baseball around."

"Where?"

"We go down the street to a little park most Saturdays."

"I don't have a ball or a glove, but I'd love to go with you if it's all right with you."

Tim said, "Perfect. When can we go?"

Billy answered, "I'm ready now if you guys are."

Ed jumped up off the floor, ran to a corner of the room, picked up a ball and glove, and said "I'm ready." The other boys ran to the same corner, grabbed their gloves, and followed Ed and Billy out the door.

They walked a long block to the park and threw for a couple hours. Billy looked at Tim and asked, "You all right Tim? You look a little tired."

"Yeah, we usually only do this for an hour or so."

Billy smiled. "I think I'll walk around and look at Strick for a while."

Robert asked, "You want company?"

"I sure do. You want to come, Ed?"

"No, I think I'll go back home with Tim."

Robert looked at Billy and grinned. "This'll be like old times, right?"

"Pretty much." Billy grinned too.

Robert and Billy walked across Strick in both directions. They talked all the way, as Billy noted businesses that might hire workers. He and Robert didn't get back to their mom's house until near dusk. They all went to church the next morning not far from the Carmichael place, and the next day Billy went back to some of the businesses he saw on Saturday, to ask for work. Each gave him one of three responses: (1) 'We don't need anybody right now.' (2) 'Get Kitty Carmichael to recommend you, and we'll hire you.' (3) 'Our hands are tied because we don't want to get on the bad side of Kitty Carmichael, and she hasn't mentioned you.'

Billy gave up on finding a job inside Strick and on Tuesday went out of town to farms in the area. He found a temporary opportunity quickly, and then others, but held out for something permanent. He walked all day, and didn't find a job he really wanted, so Wednesday morning he went back, accepted one of the temporary jobs, and worked on several different farms for the next two years. He worked every day during spring planting and during harvest, but only sporadically in between. He saved some money during his busy times, but used much of it during the slow times. He continued to live with his mom, to look at help wanted ads in the *Strick Independent* each morning, and to talk with his brothers as often as he could. He talked more often with Robert than with the others. He said to Robert one day as they sat on the front step of the house, "I want to find a good enough job I can offer Mom and you boys adequate financial security, even if not equal to that provided by Kitty. I can't even *try* to persuade Mom or you guys to move out of Kitty's house until I can provide something near equal, or until Mom thinks I have a reliable commitment. I haven't made a lot of progress with either."

Robert spoke quickly, "I trust you enough to move out of Kitty's house today, Billy, even if you offer me nothing but a tent or a barn to live in."

"I appreciate that Robert, but I didn't come here to bust up my family. I first came to add the missing link—me—and now I want to strengthen the family, not break it apart. You know what I mean?"

"Yeah, I know, and you're right. But there's no changing Mom."

"I'm afraid you're right too, but I'll try from time to time. I'm not prepared to try today, though."

Janet stuck her head out the door and said, "There you are. Dinner's ready."

Billy saw a help-wanted ad in the paper about a clerk in a hardware store, answered it, and Clyde Evans, the owner, hired him (after he checked with Kitty Carmichael), to start Monday, February 1, 1904 at $1.30 an hour for six, ten hour days a week, with a liklihood of a raise to $1.35 within a year. He'd earn almost $80 a week! He thought he'd soon be able to afford a house and could offer a better place to his mom. It turned out he didn't like the indoor, almost sedentary work, but thought it the best he could do, and he stayed with it.

Kitty provided Janet with the *New York Times* and *Boston Herald* newspapers. Billy often read parts of the latter before he went to work; one section of the paper reported admissions to various hospitals in Boston, and said a person called Susan Little entered Boston City Hospital for "starvation" on September 8.

Billy'd saved some money, and planned to save more to buy a house, but reasoned if Susan Little was *his* Susan, then he must do anything he could to meet any need she had, even though she belonged to someone else. He wrote a postcard to 'Susan Little,' C/O the hospital. He wrote on the card, *Are you Susan Little, formerly of Sinfe County,*

Missouri? If you are, I can send you and Mr. Little a small amount of money for food. Please respond. Billy Thomas.

Billy didn't expect an answer, but five days later, on September 13, he received *two* letters. Susan wrote, *I'm afraid we've each disappointed the other. I can't accept money, but maybe we can meet someday. Love, Susan.*

The other letter, signed Mildred MaHaskey, Nurse, filled two handwritten pages. It said, *Susan needs you desperately. She has no one, but I don't know how she'll react to you. I think she loves you and hates you by turns. I don't know why she does either, but maybe you do. The police brought her in, near death, nothing but skin and bones. She didn't talk a lot about her personal life, but if she had a job, it must have been a poor one; I think she gave every scrap of food she could buy to her baby, and ate nothing herself. I don't know if she has a place to live, or if she lives on the street. I would have already died, but she's young, has her baby to live for, and somehow pulled through. She's starting to get some strength back now, and I'm sure the hospital will discharge her when she gains a pound or two. She really, really needs you. I hope you'll come, and that she'll accept you. I don't know where she'll be, but come here and ask for me. Wherever she is, I'll find her. And by the way, if you write again, write to her, C/O me, not to me directly. As above, if she's not here, I'll make sure she gets your letter.*

Billy read both letters, tried to rejoice over the "Love, Susan" at the end of her letter, but didn't understand references to the baby. He didn't want to quit his job, his first decent-paying one, but he also didn't want to delay if Susan "needs (him) desperately." He decided to take time for another letter exchange. He went to the post office for a stamp, to a store for an envelope and paper, and then mailed the letter at the post office that very evening, addressed to her, C/O Mildred Mahaskey. He thought he should not tell Susan Nurse Mahaskey wrote to him, but he thought he had to know about the baby, and thought she might surmise it because of the way he addressed the letter. He wrote in his letter: *Dear Susan: Maybe I've disappointed you, but you haven't disappointed me. I still love you, even though you now belong to another man. As I said before, I have a little money—not much, but a little—and will travel to Boston to see you and Mr. Little if you think I should. I'll also help out with food if you permit me to come. I've heard a rumor about a baby. Can you tell me more? Love, Billy.*

Billy did expect an answer to his letter this time, and early the next day, Wednesday, he asked, "Mom, did you know Susan has a baby?"

Janet blushed, looked away, and asked, "How did you . . . Whatever are you talking about, Billy?"

"Did you?"

Janet continued to look away from Billy. "I already told you I don't know anything about Susan, and I don't. Why don't you just forget about her?"

"Whatever you say, Mom." Billy arose from the table and went to work, but continued to suspect his mom knew something about Susan she refused to tell him.

A letter from Susan arrived the following Tuesday, written on Boston City Hospital stationery. Susan wrote much more this time. *Dearest Billy: You'll never know how glad I am you want back in my life. I supposedly married Little—Little Little people called him—after my parents died, mainly because I had nowhere to live. Little Little has a twin called Big Little. The two shut me in a coffin-like box, shipped me to a distant place—Boston it turned out—and then locked me in a bare room not much bigger than a large closet, with not even a window. One or both of them came in periodically—every day, I suppose—with food. They'd watch me eat, make me strip, beat me with a riding crop because I used a corner of the room as a bathroom, and usually force themselves on me. I became pregnant, and had Mary Lynne—that's the name I gave her, it's not officially recorded anywhere—on the floor of the little room. I don't know if she's Little Little's or Big Little's daughter, but I love her dearly. More about her below. The Littles saw the messy room after I had Mary Lynne, beat me, locked the door again, and disappeared. I waited*

73

for a time, then beat on every wall with the tin plate I ate from, and kept it up for what might have been hours or days. A mean-looking woman in a nightgown came in and scolded me for waking her in the middle of the night, but she let us out. Mary Lynne and I lived like animals. We didn't have a real place to live or real food to eat. I hung out behind a restaurant downtown early in the evening, went through the scraps they threw out when they closed, then moved up the street a couple of blocks to a hot dog stand. The man who ran it tried to chase me off the first few nights, but then would sometimes give me a whole hot dog. More often, he'd just throw whatever he had left into a garbage can, and I'd usually find something to eat there. At first I ate everything I found, so I could nurse Mary Lynne. I'm not sure how old she is, but I weaned her, stopped eating food myself, and gave everything to her. That worked until I collapsed on a street and the police found her playing around some horses' feet. They took her to Massachusetts Manor. It's an <u>orphanage</u>! They took me to a charity place, Boston City Hospital. I'm better, but I don't think I'll ever get Mary Lynne out of that dreadful orphanage on my own. That's where you could come in, if you're willing. If you'll marry me or stay married to me—you're not married again yet are you?—and get a job here, then perhaps we can convince the orphanage people we're able to make a home for her. I know she's not your daughter, but she's my priority. I love her as much as I love you. If you'll help me, I'll be the best wife you can imagine, forever. Love, Susan.

Billy read the letter from Susan, walked immediately to the post office, bought a post card, wrote, *I'm coming,* and mailed it.

Next he walked home, told his mom he planned to go to Boston and might not come back. His mom cried, told him she believed everything he ever said, she knew about Susan, would forego her sister Kitty's protection any day for his, and she wanted to remain in his life. He didn't answer, but pulled all his money from the spot in the corner he kept it. He went to the hardware store and quit his job. Clyde tried to persuade him to stay, until Billy explained why, and then Clyde told him to use his name as a reference if he ever applied for another job. Billy went to the train station and bought a ticket to Boston's Haymarket station, a place he'd never heard of. He waited all night and until about eight the next morning for a train to Boston, showed up in Boston before his post card could be delivered, and asked directions. He walked less than three miles to Boston City Hospital, went in, and asked for Nurse MaHaskey. A badly dressed old lady told him to wait in a chair, so he did. After about five minutes, a chubby, gray-haired, motherly woman approached, and said, "Yes?"

"I'm Billy Thomas looking for Susan Little. Are you Nurse MaHaskey?"

The woman beamed. "Yes, I am. And I know where Susan is right now. She's at my house taking a nap. I'll tell you how to get there." She gave directions, and Billy left within seconds. The nurse lived only about two blocks from the hospital, so Billy walked there in a short time. He stepped up onto the front porch, swallowed hard, and knocked. He waited a few seconds and knocked again, harder. He had a history of knocking on doors, only to be greeted by strangers, and wondered if that would happen this time. It didn't. The door opened, and in front of him stood frail, skinny, blank-faced, and sleepy-eyed Susan. Her blank look remained only for a fraction of a second; then she brightened her face with a tremendous smile marred only by the absence of two front teeth, opened her arms, came out onto the porch, and kissed Billy all over his face. He longed to take her in his arms and kiss back, but knew Susan had a husband, and thought it improper. So he asked, "Should we go inside?"

"Oh, where are my manners? Yes, this isn't my house, but do come in."

"Is anyone else here?"

"No, no one."

"Susan, I didn't run away that night in Sinfe County. Arch got his pistol on me, and took me against my will." He went on and told Susan the entire story.

"Oh Billy, that's terrible. And I thought all the time you didn't like me and ran away. Our pasts aren't that different, are they? Do you still want me after I've had a Little baby?"

"Do I? I want you desperately, Susan, but of course I can't have you, because you're married to the Little guy."

"I might not be, Billy. The so-called ceremony was done by Big Little. It was weird, and it might not even have been legal. It was more like a kidnapping than a wedding. I didn't sign a marriage license like you and I did. Big Little said he'd annul my marriage to you, and offici-ate at the wedding to his brother. It happened right there in Riverbeach not more than three blocks from the courthouse, but immediately after, they put me in that horrid box, nailed a lid on it, and shipped me off to Boston. If they rode the same train they didn't have time to record anything at the courthouse, and I think they did ride the same train, because I heard them talking and laughing when they took me off, right after I got here."

"They did bring me clean men's overalls and a clean shirt oc-casionally, but no underwear, and they watched me change. Nurse Mahaskey gave me these clothes," she pointed at herself, "plus one set of underwear, shoes and socks." She paused, then continued. "When we escaped the Little room, I had the overalls and shirt, but Mary Lynne remained naked. It's really lucky we got away before winter, but I found a set of clothes for Mary Lynne at a charity clothes closet, and the Manor provided a couple of little jumper outfits."

Billy had some interest in the clothes talk, but more about Little. "You say you 'might not be' married to Little. If I can find him, I'll take him to the police, arrange a divorce if you need one, and maybe we'll never see him again. Do you know where he is?"

"That's the thing, Billy. I don't."

"Well, there's no way to know for sure, then."

"Yes, I think there is a way, Billy. If you have enough money left, you can send a telegram to the courthouse in Riverbeach, and ask. Do you have that much left after coming here?"

"Oh yes. I have enough for that and to rent an apartment and live there for a couple of months; then if I get a job, we can live there forever. Do you know where a telegraph office is?"

"The closest one I know is at the Haymarket train station. I'll go with you, and we can plan exactly what the telegram will say as we walk."

"Should we go by the hospital and tell Mildred Mahaskey where you are?"

"I'll leave her a note."

"Be sure to leave the door open to return, so to speak, because we may not get an answer to the telegram today."

"If it's as clear-cut as I think, they should be able to answer within seconds. I know where a good, but cheap apartment building is, right around the corner. Should we go rent a place on the way?"

"Let's wait and see what a return telegram says. We mustn't live together unless we're really married. If we do, it could harm our effort to get Mary Lynne back."

"But Billy, I know what the telegram will say, and the faster we get settled, the faster we can get her out of that orphanage. I know the orphanage people only want the best for her, but I want her too!"

"If the telegram says what you think it will, it will slow us down a day at most. Surely we can live with that."

"I don't want to, but you could be right. Let's say you are, and we'll wait."

They walked to the telegraph office, sent the telegram, and decided to wait up to an hour. They received a negative reply about both the Little marriage and the annulment. Billy threw his hat in the air, hugged and kissed Susan, and yelled, "Let's go rent that apartment!"

They did rent it, and because darkness fell by that time, decided to visit the orphanage first thing the next morning.They went into the apartment they rented, and Susan said, "I know you've already seen the scars on my face and the gaps in my teeth, but I want you to see what else the Littles did." She turned her back to Billy, took off her blouse and underwear, and let both drop to the floor.

Billy stared. The formerly flawless skin on her neck and back looked like one solid scar, criss-crossed with red welts. One scar even went up onto her head and took out a little strip of her beautiful brown-blonde hair. He couldn't speak. She held her arms out parallel to the floor and slowly rotated a couple full turns. Her entire upper body, including her upper arms, looked fully as bad as her back. He asked, "How did you . . . nurse Mary Lynne?" She said, "It hurt—a lot—at first, but I loved—*love*—Mary Lynne. She's worth more to me than mere momentary comfort." She put her blouse back on and started to cry. "The really bad thing is, I'm afraid you won't want me now that I have the Little's baby, and now that I'm so ugly."

She cried more, and Billy took her in his arms and held her. He stroked her hair and said, "Forget that fear. I've wanted you since before I can remember, and the intensity of my want is bigger every day. Arch couldn't beat it out of me, and Little couldn't steal it from me. I don't expect that to ever change. I feel like a winner, and I don't know how it happened. Little Little could have had you, and I don't know why he didn't go all out. But because he didn't, I won! You're the most beautiful woman in the world." She continued to cry, but Billy held her until she relaxed and then he held her longer, until she giggled and struggled to get away. Billy grinned. "Besides, I have scars too, and our teeth match. We're stuck with each other. I'll show you my scars." He took his shirt off and turned slowly around as Susan had done, so she could see.

"Wow! We do almost match, don't we! I love you, Billy. I love you because you came to find me, and for so many other reasons."

"Like what other reasons?"

"First Corinthians, chapter thirteen, lists a bunch. That chapter says charity, or love, never fails, and endures all things. I think that's my favorite, and you're a perfect example of it; there's also a poem by Elizabeth Barrett Browning, called 'Let me count the ways,' or something like that, which by itself is a good start! I'm so sorry I didn't endure all things for you. I could have moved in with your mother; she and I could have supported each other, but I knew I'd be mainly a burden at first, what with the loss of you and of my parents, so I married Little. When he proposed marriage, he promised we'd live in Riverbeach and he'd take me in a buggy twice a week to see your mother. Ha! That turned out to be a bad joke. In a way, I wish I'd never met Little. But I know I'd not have Mary Lynne today if I hadn't met him, so maybe all things, even terribly unpleasant things, do work together for good for God's children."

Billy nodded.

They entered the orphanage at eight am the next morning. The young, slender, naive-looking girl at the front desk recognized Susan, and said, mostly as a question, "I suppose you want to see Mary Lynne?"

Billy responded, "Yes, but first we want to see the head person here."

The girl shook her head. "Miss Squires doesn't normally arrive before noon, and in any case, doesn't see outsiders, ever."

Billy stepped forward a step, and said quietly, "She'll see us. We'll wait until noon, or through Friday, or through next week, or however long we have to wait. Be sure to tell her we're here when she comes in."

The girl shook her head again. "I'll tell her, but nothing will happen."

Billy stepped forward another step, opened his mouth, and felt Susan's hand on his arm. He stepped back, closed his mouth, opened it again, and spoke to Susan. "Let's find a chair to wait in."

"Perhaps we can see Mary Lynne first."

"Good idea. Can we see her right here, for all day?"

"Yes, this is the place, and I'm not aware of a time limit."

"Well, ask the girl to bring her out."

The girl brought Mary Lynne, who seemed afraid of Billy at first, but warmed up to him after an hour or so. They played with her until noon, then for another hour, and then for another. Eventually, at half-past two, the girl beckoned to Susan and said, "Miss Squires will see you now. Follow me."

The girl led all three of them into an office behind her desk, and said, "Miss Squires, this is Susan Little and . . ."

Billy finished up the sentence. "Billy Thomas."

Squires, a sour-looking person of indefinite age and gender, looked coldly at Billy and asked, "Why are you here?"

Susan answered, "Billy's my real husband. Mr. Little, however, is Mary Lynne's father."

Squires almost spat out the next words, "So where is Mr. Little?"

Susan merely shrugged, and Squires continued, "What is it you want from me?"

Susan answered with words this time. "We're a family now, we have an apartment, we can make a home for Mary Lynne, and we want to take her out of the orphanage."

"Where do you work, Mr. Thomas?"

Susan answered again, "He'll look for a job tomorrow, but he's got money already. We want Mary Lynne today."

"Anybody can say they intend to look for a job. Bring Mr. Little here, ask for Jane McIntosh, and she'll talk to you about it."

Billy responded, "We don't know where Mr. Little is, but you don't want him here. He's a really bad man. We can promise to change Mary Lynne's name to Thomas if you want, but we want her today."

"I'm afraid that's quite out of the question, Mr. . . ."

"Thomas. And we can wait right here in your office until you change your mind."

"Impossible." Squires raised it's voice. "Becky?" The girl they met out front came into Squires' office. "Call Officer Woodhouse please."

Billy sat on the floor in front of Squires' desk, opened his arms, and Mary Lynne toddled over. He said, "I bet you need a nap about now." She laid her head on his shoulder and fell asleep before Officer Woodhouse arrived.

Officer Woodhouse stood at least six feet tall, weighed over two hundred pounds, was bald, disheveled, coverall-clad, and not very talkative. He asked a one-word question. "What?"

Squires started to answer, but Billy cut him/her off. "My wife and I want to take Mary Lynne home with us, but Grouchy-Wouchy over there, wants you to say we can't."

Officer Woodhouse looked helpless, then said, "That's up to you three to decide."

Billy jumped in again, "Good, we've decided. We'll go now." He stood, still holding Mary Lynne, and headed for the office door.

Squires raised his/her voice a few decibels and an octave, and yelled, "Not so fast. If we don't fill out all the proper paperwork, the police will find you, and will bring your kid back here."

Billy continued toward the door. "Paperwork might matter to you, but not to us. Mary Lynne matters to us, we have her, and we'll keep her."

Squires looked at Woodhouse, and asked, "Officer?"

Woodhouse repeated his initial question. "What?"

"Stop them."

"I don't carry a gun; I can't shoot them. They're out the door anyway."

"Well, run in front of them and lock the outer door. They must not get away."

"Too late. They're out on the street now." Officer Woodhouse left the orphanage, went to the street, and turned the opposite way Billy and Susan did.

Susan scolded Billy. "Well, you got her for now, but you know that horrid woman won't give up. She'll send somebody after us."

"We've both been captives, Susan, and we didn't like it. Do you suppose Mary Lynne likes it better than we did?"

"I know she hates it, but I still think we should have played along with Miss Squires."

"We could have played along for years. I'll get a job tomorrow, and we'll stick around for a year or more, but I don't expect anybody to show interest in Mary Lynne, except us."

"I hope you know."

"Me too!"

No one showed up that evening to demand Mary Lynne, and Billy instructed Susan the next day, "Lock the door in case anyone shows up to take Mary Lynne. I don't expect anybody, especially on a Saturday, but I'm gonna go out and look for a job."

He went into Alperstein Hardware, only a few blocks east of the apartment, and asked a shelf-stocker about work there. The man said, "You want to talk to Mr. Alperstein. I'll find him."

Alperstein showed up and Billy said, "I'm looking for work. I already have hardware store experience and a reference." He told Mr. Alperstein about his work in Strick and told him how to find Clyde Evans.

Alperstein said, "I do need a clerk. I once met Clyde at a convention, and will send a telegram to him. Pending a favorable report from him, you'll probably get the job. I pay $1.20 per hour, with Saturdays and Sundays off."

Billy went back to the apartment and suggested they all go to a restaurant for an early lunch, then to a playground in a nearby park, and finally to a grocery store to buy a bunch of food. Susan resisted. "What if somebody comes for Mary Lynne while we're gone?"

"They won't find her. Do we care?"

"Shouldn't we?"

"I can't see why. I don't expect anybody—nobody at the orphanage knows where we live—but if they come, they'll come again." Billy grinned big, exposed his lack of teeth, and gloated, "You're the one borrowing trouble now! And besides, you need to fatten up—a lot!"

They went, then Susan put Mary Lynne down for a nap, left her with Billy, and briefly visited the hospital to tell Nurse Mahaskey at the hospital where she now lived. When she returned, Billy suggested they pray for God's love and His guidance. Susan agreed, and Billy preceded the prayer with, "Jesus said the greatest two commandments are to love God and to love our neighbor as ourselves, and if family members

aren't neighbors, who is?" He added, "If we don't remember those commandments, we can't properly love each other." They prayed, he got
the hardware store job, they lived in the apartment through March and
into April of 1905, and didn't hear again from the orphanage. Billy sent
his mom a Christmas card near the end of 1904. He included a note to
invite her to bring the boys, to help Susan and him find a house they
wanted Billy to buy for them, and then to occupy it while Billy and Susan continued to live in the apartment. He didn't mention he'd need to
borrow part of the money for a house, but his mom sent a short letter
back and declined. She added she hoped they were all well.

Susan talked often about her desire to return to Sinfe County,
but Billy always pointed out he had no farm, no livestock, no equipment, and thus no way to make a living. Susan then always responded
that Fiskur, Riverbeach, Tranberg, and other towns in the area had
hardware stores very similar to the Alperstein store.

CHAPTER NINE

Susan and Billy
Return to Sinfe County

April 1905

SUSAN INSISTED AGAIN she didn't want Mary Lynne to grow up a Little, and also didn't want her to grow up in a big city. Billy argued he had a stable job in Boston he didn't want to leave, but on Friday the fourteenth of April, he mailed a postcard to his mom in Strick, told her he, Susan, and Mary Lynne planned to return to Sinfe County to live, and invited her to bring the boys and join them; he promised to pay the train fare and to pay apartment rent until he could buy a house for them. She wrote back and turned the offer down. She said all three boys were in high school, enjoying it, and Robert had an after school job at Clyde Evans' hardware store where Billy once worked. She didn't want to disrupt all that. So Billy went to the train station and bought tickets for his family of three, from Boston to Fiskur, Missouri, and planned to formally adopt Mary Lynne and change her name to Thomas, in Sinfe County. The trip would begin on Monday the twenty-fourth, and take parts of three days, but Billy and Susan were young, at twenty-four and twenty-three years. They thought Mary Lynne, at almost two, could also handle the trip.

Billy worked through Friday the twenty-first, felt slightly feverish the last day, had moderate diarrhea on Saturday and Sunday, but felt better on Monday, and they departed as scheduled. Mary Lynne, however got sick Monday afternoon, very sick during the night, and had a high fever by morning. They were west of Allentown, Pennsylvania when Susan said, "Billy, Mary Lynne feels really hot—we've got to stop and take her to a doctor." Billy walked to the back of the train and persuaded the conductor to let them get off, then get back on Friday, at no price increase. They left the train in a little town and located a doctor. Susan took Mary Lynne there while Billy tried to find a place to stay for a few days.

He went into a run-down hotel near the railroad tracks and asked a man behind a desk, "You have an empty room I can rent for four nights?"

"Nope."

"You have anything I can rent for one night?"

"Nope."

"Do you know another place in town I can try?"

"Nope."

He departed the hotel, knocked at a nearby house with a sign outside that read, "ROOMS," and tried again.

A lady came to the door, shook her head, and said, "We're full up," before Billy could ask.

Instead, he asked, "Do you know of any place in town three of us can stay four nights?"

"No . . . well, maybe. You might try Tom Green at McPherson School. He's on the board there, and might rent the schoolhouse just outside town to you. School's been out over a week, so he might do it. Tom lives down at the end of this street, on this same side and works nights, so he might be home."

Billy found Mr. Green, and asked, "Will you rent the McPherson school building to me for four nights, starting tonight?"

"Why?" Billy explained. The man said, "Sure. If you'll sweep out the building and clean out the horse barn, you won't have to pay any rent. There's a broom in the cloak room and a manure fork in the horse barn."

Billy answered he'd do it, but then asked, "Aren't there other board members you ought to check with?"

"There's two others, but I call the shots out there. They go along with whatever I say. Go jump in the middle of it when you're ready."

"Thank you sir. We'll be there as soon as the doctor lets my wife and daughter leave his office."

Billy went back to find Susan and Mary Lynne. He'd spent several hours looking for a place, so his family remained in the doctor's waiting room. Susan commented, "I'm not crazy about a schoolhouse, but I understand you can't find anything else."

Billy answered, "Well, at least Mary Lynne saw a doctor, and if she gets worse tonight or tomorrow, we can go back."

"Yeah. The doctor said to make sure Mary Lynne has plenty to drink. He thought she'd be fine in a couple of days. I hope he knows."

"Me too."

Billy went back to town, bought a tub to bathe in, bought milk for Mary Lynne, and bread for Susan and him. Water came out of the well cold, so they pumped the tub full, let it sit in the sun a few hours, and it became tolerable. They lived in the schoolhouse the remainder of the day, for three more days, and for a total of four nights. The doctor's prediction didn't prove out completely; Mary Lynne didn't recover in two days, but got better, and seemed fine on Thursday, the third day. Billy inquired almost hourly about how Susan felt, but she felt good throughout the entire time. They went to the train station on Friday morning, and Billy spoke to the agent there. "We're supposed to get on the train west through here, today."

"You got tickets?"

"We have torn-in-two tickets. The conductor on the train Tuesday said we could get off here, and get back on today without paying extra."

"He did, did he? He didn't tell me nuthin' about it."

"Well, look at these tickets. They say Boston to Fiskur. Is this town either one?"

"Yeah, I see the tickets. How do I know you're goin' to Fiskur? It'd cost less to go from here to Boston."

"Look, Mr. . . . what's your name?"

"None o' your business."

"Oh, I see by your nametag you're Mr. Ken Malone. Well, Mr. Malone, as I understand what you said, you think we bought tickets in Boston to Fiskur, rode the train to here, and now want to go back to Boston? Why would we want to do that? Or if we bought tickets in Fiskur to Boston, and wanted to go to Boston, why would now we want to go west?"

"Yore talkin' nonsense, Boy. But I'll flag the train down, you can get on it, and straighten it out with whoever jumps you about it."

"Thanks, Mr. Malone."

They boarded the train and arrived in Fiskur on Sunday afternoon, the last day of April. As soon as they got off, Billy asked, "Should we find a place to live first, or for me to work first?"

Susan answered, "We need to live someplace starting this minute. You can go a few days without work if you must, so I think we find a place to live today, and you start to look for work tomorrow."

"You're probably right. I'll go inside the little building here and ask the guy inside."

Billy went inside to see the agent. He asked, "Do you know a place for rent in town where we might live?"

"I sure do. I have an upstairs apartment on Acorn Street that's empty right now. I'll tell you how to get there, and my wife'll rent it to you."

"Can you tell me a little about it, and how much it costs?"

"My wife decides the cost, and she'll tell you. You can also see it for yourself when you get there."

Billy went back outside, reported the conversation to Susan, and asked, "You think we ought to go check it out?"

"It sounds like the agent might be hiding something, but we have nothing else to check, so why not?"

Billy walked inside to tell the agent—Sam Mesker, a person he'd met years earlier—they'd go look. Sam wore slacks and a sport shirt. He appeared average in every way—height, weight, complexion—still looked middle-aged, but had added a trim gray mustache and his formerly black hair had developed streaks of gray. He smiled and gave Billy a sort of a business card made of one piece of hammered tin with irregular lettering; it showed Sam's full name, *Samuel A. Mesker, S. A. M.*, and told where he lived, *305 South Acorn Street*. He verbally added his wife's name, Jane.

They walked about four blocks to the address on the 'card,' knocked, and a short, thin, middle-aged woman answered.

Susan asked, "Are you Jane Mesker?"

"Yes?"

Susan explained, "Your husband sent us to look at an apartment here."

"Please come on in and have a look." They went in through the east front door and saw a large room in front of them and to their left, with two double beds and several chairs in it. They could see a bit of a room beyond, but they also saw a short stair on their right, headed west up to a landing.

Jane directed, "Just go on up the stair, and I'll be right behind you." They climbed to the landing and saw another stair, up to the south. They continued, and came into a room identical to the downstairs one, except it had no furniture in it. They walked through that room into a small kitchen containing a sort of a short pie safe with a gas oven in the lower part, a short table with a metal top with white porcelain on it, and with a moveable two-burner coal oil cooktop on the table. They didn't see a sink, drain, or water source. Susan asked about those. Jane answered, "There's a well out back. You'll need a water bucket. Previous renters just threw dish water and bath water out the kitchen window, as we do."

Jane offered the apartment at a price Billy and Susan both thought affordable, they rented it, and moved in—that is, they carried in their two suitcases and occupied the space.

The apartment had no bed for Mary Lynne, but Susan had a blanket in each of their suitcases, and she spread the two out on the floor as a pallet, and put her down for a nap. She planned for Billy and her to sleep on the bare floor until they could afford a bed for Mary Lynne.

Billy said, "I saw newspapers for sale at the train station. I'm gonna go back there and buy one. Maybe somebody has a help-wanted ad in it." He went back. Sam, as he told Billy to call him, paid for the paper and gave it to Billy.

When Sam came home from work, he climbed the stairs and knocked on the Thomas door. Susan opened it, and Sam barged in without even asking. He looked around, and asked "Don't you-all have a bed?"

Billy answered, "We plan to get one soon for Mary Lynne. Susan and I will sleep on the floor for a month or so."

Sam shook his head. "Jane and I have an extra downstairs. We'll move one up here for a few months, for you to use, with covers and pillows included. But we'll insist you and your wife sleep on it, not the kid. We don't want to get it back with stained sheets." Sam smiled.

Billy answered again, "You don't have to do that, Sam. I don't even know how we can thank you for the offer."

"Don't try. I'll come up after supper and get you to help me take the bed apart and carry it up the stairs. Speaking of supper, Jane's cooking extra for you tonight. She'll have it ready at seven. Don't be late." Susan then tried to thank Sam, but he already had gone out the door and started down the stairs.

The Thomases and Meskers became acquainted over a meal, and Billy and Susan enjoyed both the meal and the company. Jane invited them to visit the Baptist Church on Pinond Street the next Sunday. They did, and they joined it.

Billy told Susan he'd look for work Monday morning, and if he found a job, might not be back home until six or seven in the evening. He walked to Wagner Brothers Hardware, "You-all need to hire anybody right now?"

"No, but you might try Clark and Sharp Lumber. They're looking for somebody I think."

He already knew the location of Clark and Sharp Lumber, so he went, found the manager, and asked the same question: "You-all need to hire anybody right now?"

The manager looked him over, and said, "Yeah, we do. Can you lift lumber, and load it all day every day?"

"I sure can. You want to see?"

"How about we hire you, then at the end of today you tell us if you want to come back tomorrow, and we tell you if we want you."

"Does that mean I can start right now?"

"Yeah."

"Great. What do you want me to do?"

"Don't you want to know what we pay?"

"What do you pay?"

"A dollar a hour."

"What do you want me to do?"

"You'll work in the back, loading wagons for people. I'll show you where everything is." Billy went to work within a couple hours of the start of his hunt!

He and Susan debated two big questions during their first week in Fiskur. He kicked off one of them on Wednesday after he came home from work. Should they invite Billy's mom to travel there, and what costs should they offer to bear? Billy thought they should invite her, and should pay most or all the costs. He argued, "Mom doesn't have any money or a job, and depends completely on Aunt Kitty. She needs to get out of there as soon as she can, and needs us to help with the money part."

Susan countered, "You've asked her to join us before, and she won't. But in any case, we can't afford to give our money to her."

"Maybe we could invite Kitty too. I don't like her, but Mom does, and maybe it will help. Kitty might even put up some of the money."

"Well, I don't know your Aunt Kitty, but from what you've said about her, your thinking's gone off the deep end."

"Maybe it'll be good to invite Mom, even if we don't think she'll come."

"No, Billy . . . I love your mom probably as much as you do, but I love you too, too much to stand idly by and watch you do something that dumb."

"What if we sleep on it, and then I send a letter tomorrow?"

"No, Billy . . . well, maybe, but you know nobody'll come."

"I don't know that, but if you do, then what are you worried about?"

"There's always a chance . . . well, maybe nothing. Invite them if you think you must."

"Thanks, Susan. So I invite Mom, Robert, Ed, Timmy, and Aunt Kitty? And say I'll pay for the train ride and buy a small house for them after they get here?"

"Do what seems best to you."

Billy walked by the post office on his way to work the next morning and mailed the invitation letter to his mom. That evening Susan started the second debate. "Billy, we've been here almost a week, and we haven't done anything about you adopting Mary Lynne."

"Yeah, we need to start on that. One thing we might need to know is her birthdate, but you already said you don't know it. What's your best estimate?"

"I have no idea, Billy. Do you really think anybody will care?"

"I don't know for sure, but it seems probable to me; another question is about Mary Lynne's real father. Any lawyer'll likely want to know all about him. But back to the birthdate—why don't we just say August 7, 1903? We know that's the right year, and it might even be the right month."

"I won't lie, Billy. And we can't truthfully say we know a definite day."

"I don't like to lie either, Susan, but unless we do or unless we can persuade some lawyer to do it for us, we're probably out of luck."

"Well, I don't know what else we can do, so I'll agree to one lie, but to no more."

"So you're going to say Little Little is the dad—isn't that a lie too?"

"Not exactly. It *might* be true."

"Billy grinned. "But it might not."

Susan grimaced. "All right, two lies then. But no more."

"Let's do that one too, then. We almost know *Little* isn't his first name. Do you know his real one?"

"I heard it once, during the so-called wedding. It might be Henry . . . or Howard . . . or Hal—something that starts with an H."

"I don't suppose you know his middle name?"

"No."

"How about we claim he's Henry James Little?" We probably have to have a name."

"But we don't know that either, Billy. Why are you so anxious for me to lie about everything?"

"Because if we don't, the lawyer'll probably laugh us out of his office."

"Well, two lies hurt me, but I'll tell that many. That's all."

"Maybe we can actually know someday, but not tonight. You don't know where he lives do you?"

"No. I don't know if he's even alive."

"Do you know where he grew up?"

"No. I think his first wife had a farm up in the Missouri River bottoms near Riverbeach somewhere."

"Maybe I can ask for a day off next week and go up there and snoop around. Maybe I can find somebody who knows. "

"Will you do that Billy? I just won't tell another lie, not even to help you adopt Mary Lynne!"

"I said I'd do it didn't I? Tomorrow's Friday, and I'll ask then for Friday and Saturday off next week."

"Great. I'll take Mary Lynne and go out tomorrow to make an appointment with a lawyer for Monday the following week."

"Whoa! You need to wait until we know whether I'll learn anything."

"But I'm impatient! I want to *do* something."

Billy smiled. "I know you do and I do too. But we need to be as ready as we can be, before we talk to a lawyer. Why don't we forget about it until Friday of next week, then you can put a lunch in a paper sack for me, and I'll set out for Riverbeach."

"Well, I'll wait, but I won't forget about it!"

"I'm ready for that borrowed bed. If we buy a house for Mom, we might not be able to afford a bed for Mary Lynne for a few more weeks."

"I know, Billy. When do you think we'll hear from your mom?"

"The earliest will be Thursday or Friday of next week."

Billy received a letter from Strick, Kentucky on Thursday. Susan's impatience burst out, and she took Mary Lynne and the letter to the lumberyard where Billy worked. Billy opened it, and read, *Dear Billy, Kitty and I appreciate your invitation. Kitty felt torn—she said she'd like a new environment, but she doesn't want to give up the influence she has in Strick. If your invitation still stands in the spring of 1909 after Timmy graduates from high school, and if I still feel like it (I'll be 72 years old then), I'll consider it again. But for now, I think I should stay in Strick until the boys graduate from high school. I really appreciate the thought, but can't come before 1909.*

Billy kicked a pile of one by sixes, and said, "I really thought they might all come this time. I may never see any of them again."

Susan reached around Mary Lynne in her arms, and kissed him. She said, "Maybe we can all go to Strick in a year or two, and you can show off Mary Lynne as your own daughter."

. Billy smiled. "Yeah, maybe."

"Will you try to be back by supper time Saturday? The Meskers invited us to supper again that day."

"Yeah, I ought to be able to make it."

Billy took his sack lunch and began the long walk to Riverbeach before daybreak the next morning. He walked past plowed fields, past grassy hills populated with cattle and horses, and past other hills covered with timber. He walked past houses and barns, including Ben Wilson's. He continued walking until he arrived in Riverbeach in late afternoon. He saved his lunch to eat as an only meal at the end of the day, and asked several people how to find the Little farm. The first three didn't know, but the fourth talked at length.

"That was originally the Carter farm. Old man Carter died in about ought-ought or ought- one, and the young Little fella showed up almost the next day. He married widder Carter after only a few weeks. He warn't no farmer, but lived on the farm with'is new wife until she died less'n a year later. The farm's down-river about a mile. Somebody named Smith lives on it—I don't know if he bought it or if Little still owns it."

Billy walked northeast out of town, went about a mile, and saw a mailbox labeled *Eric Smith*. He went up the drive and knocked until a lady opened the door. He began witih his question. "Did this farm once belong to a man named Little?"

"Yes, please come in."

"Oh, I can't Ma'am, but I do have a couple more questions about Little."

"What are they?"

"Do you know Little's first and middle names?"

"Oh yes, I remember the deed. He signed it Harvey T. Little. I can fetch it out of the storm cellar if you want to see it. I don't know what the T. stands for.

"I don't need to see it. Do you know where he is?"

"No, Eric bought the farm a few years ago, and we've never seen Little since."

"Where do you send payment money?"

"Eric paid cash."

"Thank you Ma'am. Do you know who around here might know where Mr. Little is?"

"Probably not. You might try across the road and see if the old feller over there knows."

Billy walked across the road and asked the old guy rocking on the front porch, "Do you know where Harvey Little is?"

"Nope. I heared'e went to Boston, but I ain't heared nuthin' else. He'uz a' odd duck, a lazy money-chaser if ya ask me."

"Do you know anybody who might know where he is?"

"Nope."

Billy walked back toward Riverbeach, and asked at several more houses, but didn't learn any more about Harvey Little. He ate his meal on the shady side of a straw stack, and went to sleep. He awakened before dawn and walked back to Fiskur. Susan asked "Did you find out anything?"

He replied, "Yes, a little, but I'm not sure I can talk unless you get some food in me!"

Susan gave him a slice of bread with butter on it. "Now, tell me! I don't want to give you more, because we're going downstairs for supper in a couple of hours."

"His name is Harvey T. Little. Nobody seems to know where he is. That's all I know."

"I think that's enough to hire a lawyer. Maybe the lawyer'll know how to find him."

"Whatever you think, Dear." Billy sighed.

"I'll do it Monday."

Susan and Mary Lynne came to the lumberyard on Monday; Susan told Billy she had a lawyer appointment for Wednesday at one thirty pm, and she hoped Billy could get off from one to three. Billy stated his concern about too much time off so early in his tenure at the lumberyard, but agreed to ask. He asked, and received permission.

All three Thomases-to-be showed up at the lawyer's office on time on Wednesday. The lawyer inquired first about whether they could pay his fee, and Billy said they could. The lawyer then asked, "You want to adopt this child?"

Susan answered, "Only Billy. I'm already her mother."

"Are you not the father, Mr. Thomas?"

"No—"

Susan interupted, "A man named Harvey T. Little is the father. We don't know where he is."

The lawyer took off his reading glasses, looked at Billy, and said, "It doesn't matter if you know where he lives, but I have a few more questions for you." He asked some routine questions, then went back to the location question about Harvey Little. "We can just advertise in a paper—any paper, but I recommend the local *Fiskur Democrat*—and if he doesn't respond, we can go ahead."

Susan inquired, "What if he doesn't read the *Fiskur Democrat?*" Then her face clouded, and she muttered under her breath, "What if he *does*, and learns where I am?"

The lawyer didn't seem to hear Susan's second question. "So much the better. He won't object if he doesn't know."

Billy asked, "What do we do next?"

The lawyer smiled. "Write me a check."

"We don't have a bank, but we have cash. You want the amount you mentioned earlier?"

"Yes, and that will cover today's discussion. I'll want a check— or money—after every session."

"How many sessions do these things usually run?"

"Another couple at least, plus a session in front of a judge. Are you good for that?"

Billy swallowed hard and squeezed out a weak, "Yes." Then after a moment, "So what next after this?"

"Come back here in about three weeks. I'll take care of the ad in the paper, and then we can decide on next steps."

They left the office, Billy looked at Susan and said, "We have some savings, but the lawyer'll get most of them."

Susan looked embarrassed, but replied, "Mary Lynne is outgrowing her clothes. We need to get her some more right away, and come winter, she'll need shoes, a coat, hat, and mittens."

"I think we can handle that, *and* the lawyer, plus better winter shoes for all of us, more clothes for you, including a better coat, and a bed for Mary Lynne and for us. But we'll have to put a house on hold for a while."

Susan skipped, then hugged and kissed Billy "Billy, I love you more every day. And not just as a good provider, but do you remember all the reasons I told you back in the new apartment in Boston?"

"I'll never forget, and I'll never stop loving you, for all the same reasons, *and* because you're so beautiful."

They hugged, kissed, and continued until little Mary Lynne pulled on her mom's hand and said, "Let's *go*, Mommy."

The adoption became final in early July. Susan suggested they buy rail tickets to Strick, and visit Billy's mom before the end of August. She said Janet would want to see Mary Lynne, and if Harvey Little came looking, they'd be far away. Billy put up a feeble resistance. "If we do that, we'll set back a house-buying date. And I'll have to ask for more time off from work."

"Don't be stuck to a house or a job, Billy. I want to be sure Harvey doesn't find us and you want to see your family. You know it, so let's do it!"

Billy sighed but agreed, and down deep, felt happy that he did.

They went to Huntington, West Virginia in early August and Robert picked them up and took them to Strick. They had a great visit with Billy's mom and the boys, and even Aunt Kitty seemed to mellow a bit. Billy didn't mention a move to Fiskur to his mom, but did invite Robert. Robert didn't want to go. "I've got a pretty good job at Clyde Evans Hardware, and I've got my eye on a girl I want to ask out. So I think I'll just stay here."

They stayed in Strick only four days, because Billy asked for a week off, and the train ride took some time. They returned to Fiskur on Saturday afternoon, August 12, walked south toward their apartment, and Billy looked forward to a day of rest before he returned to work on Monday. However, as they approached their apartment, he heard a woman scream. He looked at Susan, yelled, "you two wait here," and ran toward the house. When he entered it, he saw Jane Mesker in a chair behind a table facing him, with Arch Smith in another chair facing her and pointing a gun at her. Arch turned around toward the door Billy slammed, flashed an evil grin, and said, "You thought you got away, didn't you, Boy. They sent me up for three years, but I'm out now, and am takin' you back. You won't slip away for even a day this time." He turned, pointed the gun at Billy, and told him to go out the door first this time.

Billy started to shake, but said, "You threatened to kill me every day for three years. You'll have to do it today this time, because I won't go with you."

Arch pulled the hammer back on his gun and pointed it at Jane again. "I ain't a shootin' you today, but I'll shoot this 'ere woman if'n you don't go out that door there." Jane turned white, Billy went, and Arch followed.

"All right, the woman's inside and you're outside. Go ahead and shoot me if you must, because I won't go another step. I know you're behind me and can do it, so I'm calling you. Just go ahead and do it."

"You better walk, Boy, 'cause if'n you don't, I'll go back inside and shoot the woman."

Billy knew that if Arch went inside, he could jump behind the corner of the house and probably get away. Instead, he walked, but in a direction he thought Arch didn't want to go. He felt Arch hit him from behind, saw stars, and knew nothing else for a time. He awoke in a bouncing, fast-moving wagon, and heard the Fiskur City Marshal yell, "Stop!"

Billy's mind remained fuzzy, but he decided to jump—or fall—out the back of the wagon, and maybe Arch wouldn't notice. He did it, but his already messed-up head hit a rock, and he passed out again.

He woke up this time in another wagon, driven back toward Fiskur by elderly City Marshal McIntire, a fat, sloppily dressed, but kind-looking man. He lifted his head and the Marshal said, "Your wife told me what you done, Son, and it was a brave thing. But next time, wait for me. I got the guy, but it'd a' been easier if you hadn't a' got mixed up in it."

"Where is the guy?"

"He's tied up right next to ya, Son. Are you all right?"

"Yeah, I'm all right. What will you do with him?"

"I dunno. It depends on if he's committed other crimes an' if he's wanted or not." Billy didn't answer, but moved as far away from Arch as he could. The Marshal asked, "Where you want out?"

"Where's my wife and daughter?"

"At Sam Mesker's house."

"Let me off there."

The City Marshal did, Susan and Jane praised Billy, and he soon went upstairs to bed. His head looked terrible but felt much better by morning. He intended to return to work on Monday, and have a more normal day. He didn't know what would happen to Arch, but he supposed it would involve more jail time, and he tried to put it out of his mind.

Fall, winter and spring came and went. A 'For Sale' sign appeared on a lot across the street from the Mesker house in June of 1906. Billy wanted the lot, and suggested to Susan, "Let's buy that lot, then continue to save money, and maybe I can build the house myself. I think Clark and Sharp will give me a little off on lumber, and I can save a labor charge if I build it myself. I hope we can do it by 1909 when Mom'll need it."

"Whatever you think, Billy."

They bought the lot, and waited until fall of 1907. Then they hired a guy to bring several wagon loads of rocks, which Billy intended to use to make a foundation. He planned a three-room house, modeled after his mom's former farmhouse, except it would face west instead of south. He hired a different man to haul lumber from Clark and Sharp, and to stack it on the lot. Unfortunately, the man stacked it on a lot over on Cantrell Street, and Becca Stern, the owner of the lot, wouldn't allow him to move it. Billy went over to talk to Becca.

"What is it you want, Becca?"

"Get off my property, or I'll call the City Marshal."

He had hoped he could learn what Becca really wanted, but she wouldn't talk to him. So he turned the problem over to the Board of Aldermen in Fiskur, and began the work of making a foundation on his own lot. The Aldermen eventually pressured Becca to let Billy haul the lumber over to his Second Street lot, but not before July of the next summer.

Billy and Sam Mesker started building the first evening after Billy hired another guy to haul the lumber, and several other neighbors also helped. They made good progress, and had the house framed before the end of July, but then vandals pulled it all down. Billy never learned who did it, and felt dumb to re-start, but he did begin again. The *Fiskur Democrat* ran an article about Billy's problem, and over three dozen men showed up before Billy went to work on Monday morning, August 3. One of the men claimed to be a house-builder. He persuaded Billy to explain what he wanted; he did and went on to the lumberyard. When he came home from work all the men except the house-builder were gone, but the house frame stood again, with the roof shingled, and with a few replacements for boards they couldn't salvage. The house-builder said the lumberyard gave them the replacements free. This time, Billy sat on the lot and watched all night for vandals, but none came. The men showed up again on Tuesday, and finished the house. It lacked only furniture. Billy knew some of the men, found one, and thanked him. Then he went to his apartment at Sam's, he and his family moved their few belongings that evening, and they stayed in the new house Tuesday night, August 4. Billy told Susan they should continue to rent the Mesker apartment, at least for most of a year, because if his mom came to Fiskur, she'd live in the new house and they'd need to go back to the apartment.

Billy's mom didn't come. He received a telegram from Robert on October the twenty-second, saying their mom suffered a heart attack on the twenty-first, hovered near death, and Billy should hurry to Strick. He and his family bought train tickets and left Fiskur that evening, but didn't make it to Strick soon enough to see Janet alive. They arrived on the twenty-fourth, but Janet died on the twenty-second. They attended the funeral on the twenty-fifth, and started home later that evening. Billy talked to Robert minutes before they went in the church for the funeral. "Thanks, Robert, for being here. I think I should've been here, but I'm confident you made all the right decisions. Thanks."

Robert remained silent a moment, and then responded. "I didn't make any decisions, Billy. Dr. Musialer made them, but it didn't matter. Aunt Kitty says Mom was gone from the first symptom of the heart attack, and she's right."

"That's probably true, Robert. Do you mind if I pray for you?"

"No, go ahead."

Billy put his hand on Robert's shoulder. *Dear God, please be with Robert. He's leader of his family now, and please don't make him do it all alone. Guide him, show him, and help him. In Jesus name I ask it. Amen.*

Robert didn't respond when Billy finished. They merely went up the church steps and into the building. But after the funeral, Billy found all the boys together and invited them to go back to Fiskur, either that day, or later. Robert answered for the three. "We really appreciate you asking, but we've grown up here in Strick. It's our home now, and we want to stay." Billy didn't want to accept that answer, but didn't argue with it, and didn't ask the boys to come to Sinfe County again.

Billy bought a separate ticket for five-year-old Mary Lynne, and after she went to sleep in her own seat, Susan touched Billy on the arm and said, "I know you're devastated, Billy, and so am I. But sometimes one life gets replaced by another"

"Yeah. Sometimes, maybe."

"Not just sometimes. This time."

"So what's that have to do with us?"

"Everything, Billy. I'm pregnant."

"You're what?"

"Pregnant. Mary Lynne's gonna have a little brother or sister!"

Billy temporarily forgot about other passengers. He yelled, "Yippee!" More quietly he said, "I wish Mom could have known; I wouldn't want to consciously make the trade, and maybe I shouldn't even say it, but I think it's a good one!" Billy hardly slept, but laughed and bubbled almost all the way home.

When they got to the train station, Billy told Sam the baby news even before he told him they no longer wanted the apartment.

Susan had a little boy on June 18, 1909, and named him William Earl. They called him W.E. Mary Lynne acted important as she 'helped' take care of him, but she started to school in September, and left W.E. to his mother for most of most days. Mary Lynne slept in the middle room of the house, the same as her parents, and Susan converted the south room to a nursery for W.E.

Billy asked, "How likely are Mary Lynne and W.E. to have another brother or sister?"

"It could happen. I'm still young, at 28. You might have a whole slew of children before you're done!" Billy grinned.

CHAPTER TEN

To Arizona and Strick

January 1911

MORE TIME WENT BY and no more children came, but W.E. turned out to have health problems. His chest became congested and his ears infected when he had a cold. Also, Billy pushed him in a swing on his first birthday, but he fell out and broke his arm. Dr. Chisholm seemed to almost live at the Thomas house. W.E. used his scant breath to cry about his ears one cold day in January of 1911, and Dr. Chisholm recommended they move to Arizona Territory for a few years. He said W.E. might grow out of his health problems, but also might not survive them in Fiskur.

Susan didn't want to take W.E. outside, so waited for Billy to come home from work, and met him at the door. "Billy, I think we need to go to Arizona, just as soon as W.E. can travel, maybe tomorrow. Dr. Chisholm recommends it."

Billy came in and sat suddenly in a chair. "What?" Susan explained, and Billy replied, "We don't have to decide today do we?"

"I've already decided. We have to go, Billy."

"Well, I might be on board with that after I sleep on it, but let me do that much, all right?"

"One night is fine, but you need to get down to the train station and buy tickets from Sam first thing tomorrow."

"Buy tickets to where?"

"Arizona Territory."

"Arizona's not even a state."

"Dr. Chisholm said Arizona. So that's where we need to go."

"Where in Arizona do you want to go?"

"Anywhere. All I know is Dr. Chisholm said Arizona."

"Is Tucson all right?"

"It's in Arizona, so it's fine."

"You're sure you want to take W.E. into a wild place like that?"

"Dr. Chisholm said Arizona. So I'm sure."

"I'll sleep on it."

"Fine, Billy. I don't mind if you sleep on it, just as long as you wake up tomorrow and do it."

Billy went to work the next day, quit his job, and then went to the train station to buy tickets to leave for Tucson the next day. He told Sam what he intended, asked him to rent his furnished house and treat it as his own—to keep the rent—and went home to help Susan pack up. They left early the next day, Susan held W.E. all the way, they made it through Oklahoma by the following morning, and to Tucson before daybreak the day after.

They got off the train and looked for a place to live. They found another upstairs apartment—two rooms again—in a house in the south part of Tucson, owned by Jose and Maria Hernandez. Billy went the next day to look for a job. He tried lumberyards and hardware stores, to no avail. He found a part-time job mixing concrete for a construction company halfway through the next week. He had to walk most of the way across town from the apartment to the north part of town to get to work. He only worked when someone didn't come in. Another employee had to come after him and then they had to walk to the job, so Billy never made it to work on time. He expected to be fired any day, but instead went to full time after about a month. He had to leave home early, and he came back late and tired, but at least he arrived for work on time.

W.E. didn't recover suddenly, and a new doctor, a Dr. Martinez, had to visit a few times, but he did improve. Susan didn't send Billy for

Dr. Martinez even one time during the second winter, and he started to talk about a return to Fiskur. Susan, however, worried. "What if he relapses when we go back? What if we can never go back?"

"How will we ever know if we don't try it?"

"Let's wait at least one more winter before we try it. W.E.'ll be almost four by then, and stronger. Besides, those awful Littles aren't likley to find us as long as we stay here."

"Well, I don't know when'll be the right time and I can protect you from the Littles there as well as here, but if you think another winter, I can mix concrete that long."

Susan kissed and hugged Billy. She said, "I love you Billy. You'll do anything for your children, and that's one reason—only one of the many!"

Billy smiled.

He sent a telegram to Sam Mesker in February, 1913. It said, *Arizona's been a state for about a year, and we expect to be in Fiskur before the middle of April.*

He bought train tickets in April, 1913. The family boarded the train in Tucson early on a Sunday morning, and arrived in Fiskur during the night after a little more than two days of travel. Sam worked days at the station, so they didn't see him, but went directly to their house to find it empty and clean. They all crashed into their beds, and slept until ten A.M.

Billy went to the train station to thank Sam, then went to the lumberyard to learn they needed no help. He went back home to rest more and to form a plan. Thursday, the next day, he inquired at businesses all over Fiskur, but found nothing. He came home discouraged, and spoke to Susan about it. "We might have to move to Tranberg or Riverbeach to find work."

"Oh, Billy. I don't want to move. Mary Lynne already started school in Fiskur, moved to Tucson, and now is back. She'll be in fourth grade and still has friends here. Isn't there anything else you can try?"

"I think I covered the town today, but I'll go out tomorrow and see if I could have missed anybody." Billy looked again Friday, but as before, found nothing. He decided to find temporary work on a nearby farm if he could, then when that dried up, look again for something more permanent. He tried every farm within a one-hour walking distance of his home on Saturday, but local farmers thought him too old and too beat-up for farm labor—already past thirty, no teeth showing, a battered face, and a knocked-down shoulder.

They went to church on Sunday. The Meskers invited them for dinner after church, and while at their house, Sam suggested a new idea to Billy. "Why don't you start your own business?"

"Like what?"

"Oh, I don't know, maybe start a livery stable or a construction business or something like that."

Billy seemed interested. "A construction business might work. I'd need money—to get land and a building—for a livery business. But will anybody hire me to build anything?"

Sam grinned. "I will. I want a workshop out behind the house." He pointed. "Why don't you work up a budget, tell me what it'll cost, and we'll go from there. And you'd better include a profit in your cost."

"Exactly where do you want it, and how big do you want it?"

"After Jane gets the pie in here and we're nice and full, we can go out and talk about it."

They went out to find Sam already had stakes in the ground. They talked details briefly, went back inside and visited for a while, then the Thomases went back across the street to their home. Susan encouraged Billy to pursue the idea. First thing Monday, he made a plan, went to the lumberyard to learn prices, and then went to see Sam at the train station. Sam had already told him what he wanted—the cost was the only thing he didn't know. He approved the plan and told him to go ahead.

Billy ordered foundation rocks, as well as lumber to be delivered, and didn't do much else on Monday, but Sam only wanted a ten by ten with a shed roof and no windows, so with Sam's help after work, he mostly finished it in two more days. On Thursday, he went back early to put the door on and to make a rock step out front. A man he barely knew, Ben Gibson, came by to talk to him. He looked taller than Billy, not much older than him, but with gray in his mustache and hair. After some small talk, Ben went to his subject. "Will you build a house for me?"

"I sure will . . . how'd you hear about me?"

"Sam Mesker and I both work for the railroad. Sam told me. I live north of the tracks in an old house, but I want to build a better one in front of it. I'll provide the lumber and anything else you need, I'll help every day after work, and my son, Ben Jr. will help after school. He's seventeen and won't know much about building, but when it comes to being strong, he's a man."

"Sounds like a deal about to happen, Ben. I'll go by after supper and look at the site. You'll be there around seven, right?"

"Yep."

Billy went, talked more with Ben about exactly what he wanted, made a few notes, and went home.

He talked to Ben after supper the next evening. "I'll do it. You say you'll provide all the materials?"

"Yep."

"Then if you like this plan," Billy handed Ben a paper with a drawing on it, "I'll work for four-fifty a ten-hour day."

"Ain't that a little steep?"

"No, not if you consider I know how to do it and will work five days a week for sure, six most weeks."

Ben shook his head, but then stuck out his hand for a shake. "All right, get to it. When can you start?"

"I can start tomorrow."

"How about you wait 'til Saturday, so I can get rocks and lumber delivered."

"Good." Billy stuck his hand out for another shake.

He went home and told Susan, who jumped up and down and said, "I never knew I'd be married to an important town businessman!"

Billy grinned and replied, "I have tomorrow off, too. Ben won't have materials ready until Saturday.

Susan kissed Billy, but a knock on the door interrupted the kiss. Billy walked to the open door and saw his big, tall, overalled neighbor, Tim McArtery there. He smiled. "Come on in, Tim."

Tim looked grim shook his head, put his hands on his massive belly, and replied, "No, you come out."

Billy went out. "What is it Tim?"

"I understand you're gonna work for Ben Gibson. That right?"

"Yes."

"You can't do that, Billy."

"Why?"

"Ben's . . . black, Billy."

"Yeah?"

"White men don't work for black people."

"This one does. But I won't involve you in any way."

"You'll never finish it."

"Why?"

"It'll burn down before you do."

"If I didn't know you better, Tim, I'd say that sounds like a threat."

"It is. And it ain't the only one. Your own house'll burn, too. With your wife and kids inside."

"I think you need to go back home, Tim. I can debate anything with anybody, until they say they'll harm my family. Then I stop talking to them. Go on home now."

"I ain't sayin' *I'll* do anything. I'm just sayin' what'll happen."

"I'm about to go back inside now. You go on home."

Billy went in, shut the door, and told Susan about his confrontation with Tim. She managed a nervous laugh, and said, "Disregard Tim. He's nothing but a big fat blowhard. Go ahead and do what you think is right; I know you will, but you have my backing."

"Let's all go to the train station and talk to Sam. I don't want to leave any of you alone, even long enough to do that."

"Good. I have some news for you, and we can talk about it on the way."

They went, and Susan told him, "I'm pregnant again, Billy. I think I might be due in about November."

"Wow! Wow! If I'm not careful, I could forget why we're headed to the train station!" After a short pause, Billy asked, "Are you sure about it?"

"I'm sure."

"Oh, Wow!"

They arrived at the train station, and Billy tried to be calm, as he talked to Sam. "Hey, Sam, you'll never guess what's about to happen to us!"

"Maybe you better just tell me then."

"Susan's pregnant again!"

Sam jumped up, reached across his desk, and shook Billy's hand. "Congratulations. I hope you have another boy. You're gonna need help one o' these days!"

"Well, Sam, on another note, maybe I need help right now. Tim McArtery came over. He threatened Susan and the children because I'm working for Ben Gibson. He scared me, and I'm thinking they ought to get out of town for a while. Can you sell me round-trip tickets for them back to Tucson for a couple of weeks?"

Sam looked grave. "You think two weeks is enough, Billy?"

"Yeah, I think Tim'll cool down by then."

"Well, I'd like to see 'em be gone longer."

"We'll try two, and see what happens."

"When you took that job, Billy, the news went through town like a grass fire in a high wind, and I don't mind telling you, the mood's ugly. I know Ben. He works for the railroad too. He's a hard worker and a nice guy. But . . . maybe you ought to cancel the job . . . maybe it's not worth it."

"You know me, Sam. I told Ben I'd build his house, and I intend to do it. If I don't, I'm telling Tim I'm his puppet to play with any time he wants."

Susan looked about to cry. "Maybe you ought to listen to Sam, Billy."

Sam acknowledged Susan's support with a nod. "Everybody except you knows it's not worth it, Billy, but if you think it is, then I recommend your family leave on the next train through here. One to the west's due in about three hours. Do you know where they can go?"

"To Tuscon, like I already said. Can you send a telegram there?"

"Sure."

Billy wrote a telegram to Jose Hernandez, asked him to save their apartment if it remained available, and turned to Susan. "Let's go home. You can pack some suitcases, and you should include anything you don't want burned up in the house."

"Well Billy, that's everything we have."

"You know what I mean."

"Not really, but let's go home and get started."

They went home. Billy pulled money from under their bed and gave it to Susan. Then he went outside and continually walked around the outside of the house until they headed back to the train station. Billy carried two suitcases, Susan carried W.E., and Mary Lynne walked beside them. Susan promised to send a telegram to tell him if the Hernandez's had a place, or if they had to look elsewhere. He waited at the station until the train came, his family boarded, and the train left. Sam looked at Billy and frowned. "You probably ought to find the Marshal and tell him to watch your house. It'll likely burn you know. In any case, I don't want to put Jane in danger by letting you move back upstairs over us."

"Yeah, I'll find the Marshal, but I think the whole thing's silly."

Billy stayed home and watched his house himself on Friday, and aside from another 'neighborly' visit, nothing happened. He went to the Gibson place and began to build on Saturday. He went back the entire next week, and thought the furor over. He received a telegram from Susan, to say they were back in the Hernandez apartment. He returned to Ben's on Monday the twenty-eighth, and about midmorning saw smoke. He ran to check and saw his own house afire, so much so that he merely turned, went back to Gibson's, and continued to build. When Ben came home from work that evening, Billy recommended someone watch the new building all night—Ben said he'd done that from the beginning—and he talked to Sam about it before Sam went home that day. He suggested, "You ought to send a telegram to Susan to tell her to stay at least another two weeks."

"Maybe I'll send one to tell her to go to Strick instead, for a full year. Robert's there, and he'll look out for her."

"Good idea. And you ought to move around from night to night—don't sleep in the same place two nights in a row."

"Can you send a telegram to Susan?"

"Yeah. What's her address?"

"It's 3117 South Rives Avenue, Tucson, Arizona."

"What do you want to say?"

We still have trouble here. I'll buy tickets to Fiskur for you and the children. Get on the train . . . "When should they get on the train, Sam?"

"The next time they can get on there will be tonight at eight -ten." *at 8:10 tonight. Stay on it when you get here, and I'll come on the train with tickets to Huntington. I'll ask Robert to pick you up, and you might have to stay a year.*

Billy decided to sleep outside by straw stacks for a while, but went back to Ben's building on Tuesday. Someone shot a bullet over his head from among some trees over to the west, about mid-morning. Because he thought the report sounded like a rifle, and because he didn't expect anyone with a rifle to miss from that distance, he thought maybe the shot could be more of a warning than an effort to kill him, but told both the City Marshal and Ben about it. He also wondered if he should tone down his "fearless" behavior, but decided if he did, he'd never build anything again. He sent a telegram to Robert to tell him Susan and the children intended to go to Huntington, and to ask if he'd rent a buggy at Billy's expense, pick them up at the train station, take them to Strick, and allow them to stay up to a year. He said Susan would explain. Robert sent a return yes.

Billy and the Gibsons had the house nearly built by mid May, when Billy took off to meet the train. He told Susan all that had happened, about his concerns for the future, and finished up with, "You and the children might have to stay in Strick for a year,
but when things settle down here, I'll come after you for sure. The whole plan stinks, I know, but it's the only way I can think of to keep you all safe."

"Well, Billy, I agree; your plan stinks, but I'm confident your judgment is good, and I'm also confident the horrid Littles won't look for us in Strick. The children and I will do it, but not for a day more than a year!"

He kissed both children, then Susan, and grinned. "I'll be there on day 364, or earlier if I can. Right now, I need to get back to Ben's house."

He ran off the train barely before it left, watched it out of town, and went back to Ben's. They finished the house on Saturday, May 18, and Ben brought up a touchy subject. "You did a good job, Billy. I'd like to find a dozen or so guys to help you rebuild your house on Saturdays, but I don't want to get you in more trouble than you're already in."

"You don't have to do that, Ben. I'm a builder, I can rebuild it, but I'm not afraid of help from you or your friends."

"Then a bunch of us'll be there Saturday, bright and early."

Billy planned to use the existing foundation for his house. He had lumber delivered, and Ben and over a dozen friends showed up on Saturday. They made a lot of progress, and every man promised to come back the following Saturday. Sunday, however, both Billy's incomplete house and Ben's new house burned; Ben had lost his wife to diphtheria several years earlier, but had three sons. The youngest, twelve-year-old Lee, suffered burns on his right arm and right leg when the new house burned. Dr. Chisholm said Lee'd have scars but no other permanent effects. Ben told Billy, "I can't afford to buy more materials right now, or to pay you, but me and my boys already moved back to the old house, and we can just stay there. What do you plan to do?"

"I can't afford to rebuild either. I don't know what I'll do." He paused, and then spoke slowly. "One thing I *won't* do is write to Susan right now and tell her about all my troubles. I don't want to worry her."

Ben looked thoughtful, then said, "You could be right. Why don't you stay with me and the boys until something jars loose for you?"

Billy didn't hesistate. "Thanks, Ben. I'll do it. I'll accept that as payment from you, and I'll help you watch for people who might skulk around the old house."

"That'll be great, Billy. Me and the boys can watch, but another pair of eyes can't hurt."

So Billy moved in with Ben, and three different friends of Ben showed up before they went to work on Monday, to try to hire Billy to do building projects. Billy looked at all the projects, made a proposal for each of them, and eventually agreed to do all three. Two of the projects were for small buildings, and one was for a house. He intended to tackle the small ones first, then to work on the house, but a lot of people showed up to help on Saturdays, and Billy finished all three on May 29. In the meantime, Billy and Ben's oldest son, Ben Jr., caught two guys trying to fire Ben's old house, and Ben Sr. and his middle son, Dave, caught two more. Billy scheduled another house, a little horse barn, and a larger hay barn for Ben's friends.

As before, a large group of Ben's friends showed up on Saturdays to help. Billy's building business boomed that summer and fall. Although the arsonists tried many times, they never succeeded. He earned enough to rebuild his house, but decided to save his money and wait until his reputation in town improved.

He did plan to go for Susan. Ben said she and the children could live with him and his boys for a while, but as he thought about when to go, he received a telegram from Kitty, on December 1, 1913. Susan'd had a little girl that morning, and had named her Janet Sue.

Billy almost couldn't contain himself. He sent a telegram: *Stay there. I'll come as fast as a train can get me there.* He bought a ticket from Sam and sent a telegram to Robert to ask him to meet him in Huntington. He didn't wait for a reply, and left that evening.

He arrived in Huntington Tuesday evening and met Robert there. They started for Strick within minutes, and arrived before Susan and the older boys went to bed. Susan took him into the kitchen of Kitty's little house, where all of Billy's children were asleep. "Look, Billy. I'm so proud of them I could just bust."

"Yeah, me too. I want to wake them all up and hug them, but I won't. Janet Sue's as beautiful as her mom. If I suddenly bust instead of you, you'll know why!"

Robert talked to his brothers. "Come on guys, let's get out of here for a while and let Billy and Susan talk. They probably want to catch up on a bunch of things."

The boys left, and Susan spoke about them. "They're a great bunch of boys, but none of them will ever be a Billy!"

Billy grinned. "Did you think they would be?"

Susan grinned too. "I hoped."

"Yeah, right!"

"Are you done with our house yet?"

"No. I came to see Janet Sue, but the house burned. It could be better if I go back and rebuild it, then you all come in a month or two."

Susan grinned again. "Look, Billy, I agreed to come out here for a year. It hasn't been quite that long on the calendar, but it's been a few decades in my mind. We're all going back with you. You may as well buy the tickets, because you can't get rid of us!"

Billy tried to look serious. "We don't have a place to live, Susan."

"Where do you live?"

"With Ben and his boys."

"We can do that too. It's been so long since Ben and his boys had a woman's cooking they probably don't even remember it. It'll be fun to watch them get used to it again. And besides that, you probably have not a beginning of a business record. It will already take me months, just to piece all your records together."

Billy answered, "Maybe, but only if house burners don't learn you're home and go after Ben's house. The records don't much matter anyway."

"Billy, you're borrowing trouble . . . again, and in two ways!"

Susan made another pallet on the kitchen floor and they went to sleep before the boys came back. Robert took them all to Huntington on Friday, and they arrived in Fiskur on Sunday. They found a light snow on the ground, but Billy said people's tracks would show in the snow, and might deter the house burners. Ben's old house had only two rooms, but he and his sons crowded into the sitting/sleeping room each night, and left the kitchen for Billy, Susan, and family. Despite a bigger snow on Sunday, Billy finished up work he'd already agreed to do, with the customary help on Saturdays. He began work on his own house Thursday. He'd barely started when Tim McArtery visited again. He had better news this time.

"When you and Ben Gibson's boy caught Tim Bolivan a tryin' to burn Ben's house, you busted th' back o' th' burnin' notions. Tim'uz th' ramrod of the burnin's. He also got a old Ku Klux Klan guy in here to talk to a bunch of us—to a bunch of guys—and he turned our—their—stomachs. He talked about hangin' people and other stuff people in Fiskur don't wanna do, and that'uz another turning point. You're looked at by a lot o' folks in Fiskur as a all right and tough guy. Not by ever'body, but by enough, I think."

"Thanks, Tim. I kind of had the idea the burning fever had broken, too. It's been several months since anyone's tried it. But what you say sounds good to me, and I'll keep on building here, with more confidence than if you hadn't talked to me."

On Saturday as well as the following Saturday, not only did a large group of people from north of the tracks show up to help Billy, but Sam, Tim McArtery, several people from their church, Pastor Javier, Ron and Gertie Knight from South Sinfe Church and Ben and Sally Wilson from near Riverbeach came—Gertie and Sally came with kettles and spits to help Susan cook for all the people.

So many people came to help build the house, and Billy had gained so much experience managing big crews, they completed the house on the second Saturday except for a few details. Billy finished on Monday, December 29, 1913. He talked to Susan and Ben about the house the day before. "I ought to be able to finish our house tomorrow, so Ben, my family'll move out then. I really appreciate your help in every way, including getting to live here, and we'll never forget it."

Ben answered, "Well, Billy, from everything that's happened and from what you've said, it seems you'll be safe over there, but I'll come every night to help you keep watch; I didn't tell you about it, but you got two houses, a little horse barn and a smoke house to build here north of the tracks just as soon as you can start."

"Wonderful, Ben. I'll start on Tuesday. Susan, can you be ready to move by noon on Monday?"

"Considering we don't have anything to move I can be ready at the drop of a hat." Susan laughed.

"I'm sorry we don't have anything, Susan, but we might have to go another month or so before we can afford to stop sleeping on the floor." Billy didn't laugh, but at least he grinned back.

They moved Monday, and during the move, Ron Knight showed up for a brief visit. He told Billy he wanted to retire, and because he'd bought Billy's farm at the tax auction, he thought he should make a proposal to him first. He said Billy could farm both farms as his own, could use the Knight equipment and livestock as his own, could live in the Knight house (because the Thomas house would require a lot of fixing up), and would owe rent only on the house. Billy said he'd think about it, but his booming business probably meant he'd eventually say no. He went back to work on paying jobs Tuesday, but that night, Billy stood outside in a shadow watching his house about an hour after he took over from Ben, and saw a short and skinny person approach the door to his house. He intercepted the person before he/she knocked, and asked, "Who are you? What do you want?"

"I'm Tim Bolivan. I'm here to tell you a bunch of us plan to hang you tomorrow, from this tree limb here," he pointed, "at exactly noon."

Billy didn't know whether to take the man seriously. So he asked again, "What'd you say your name is?"

"You heard me the first time. If you know what's good for you, you'll get out of town within the next hour."

"Mr. Bunglehead, or whatever your name is, you've lost the support of too many people. You'll never be able to pull it off."

"Ha! You don't think so? Well, then, you just be here tomorrow at noon."

"I don't think so, Mr. Stumblefoot. I'll be a few blocks north of here, building a horse barn at noon tomorrow. But I'll be sure to let the City Marshal know where he can arrest a person bent on murder."

"That's right. Hide behind the law, you coward."

"I can do that now, Fumblefingers, because public opinion has shifted. You're the guy should look over his shoulder at every shadow now. You just run on home and calm down—I know where you live, you know. I'll wait only about ten seconds before I push your ugly nose so far back in your face nobody'll ever have to see it again." Tim Bolivan's short, scrawny stature made Billy think he could do it.

Tim apparently thought the same, because he turned and hurried away. Billy didn't expect more trouble from Tim, but decided to continue to watch for a few weeks anyway; Tim didn't show up the next day, or anytime soon.

CHAPTER ELEVEN

The Jail Break

January 1, 1914

BILLY'S BUSINESS SEEMED ready to take off when the new year opened in 1914. But early on January 1, Sam came across the street with a copy of the Kansas City Times from the previous week. The paper reported the Thursday night escape of Zachariah Smith, Arch Smith, and Mort Callagher from the penitentiary in Jefferson City, along with information about rantings before the escape to suggest they might head either to places around Arch Smith's farm in Celyne County, or to the Fiskur area. The article didn't speculate about reasons for going to either location, but Billy read the report and speculated on his own.

He talked about the problem with Susan. "This is our worst nightmare. I been wondering when those guys would get out, but it didn't occur to me they might escape. We could go to Jefferson City—probably the last place those guys will be—to Celyne County to help protect the Hastings', or we could invite the Hastings' to stay with us until the criminals are caught. You have a thought?"

"Yes. How about a nice vacation to Jefferson City, where we'll all be safe."

"I probably shouldn't have mentioned that one." Billy grinned. "That one does nothing for the Hastings', and I owe them big."

"Yes, but think about Mary Lynne, W.E. and Janet Sue. You have an even bigger obligation to them, don't you think?"

"Of course, and to you, too. But I can handle more than one obligation at a time. I think I should send a telegram to the Hastings' within the hour, get them here, and we can all stay here, watch, and Will and I can drive off the bad guys if they come. They could be here any minute, you know, depending on how they travel."

"Billy, that's dumb. First, we don't have enough beds or space here. Second, Art and his buddies could destroy the Hastings' house if they're not there."

"Arch. We might be a little more crowded than we'd like, but Arch and Company could destroy the Hastings' house *and* the Hastings if they stay where they are."

"Why don't *you* go, and leave us in peace?"

"So you and the children can be here alone? Now *that's* dumb. I won't even think about doing such a thing."

Susan sighed. "Well, invite them here if you must, but the children and I won't go there. We've already been chased out of our home too many times."

"Great. I'll go to the train station and get off a telegram now." Billy ran all the way to the station and expected to find Sam, but didn't. He sent the telegram anyway, suggested the Hastings ride the train from Humphrey to Fiskur, and said he'd meet both trains from Humphrey scheduled to come that day. He thought he could leave his family for a few minutes, two times. He ran back home, felt relief to find Susan and the children fine and by themselves, settled down for an uneasy day, waited until almost time to meet the first train from Humphrey, and heard a knock on the door. He tightened his grip on his new single-shot .22, and yelled, "Who is it?"

Someone yelled back, "Telegram for Mr. Thomas."

Billy went to the door, took the telegram, and thanked the messenger, He came back inside and read it to Susan. *Will's been sick for several months, and can't travel. Thanks for the warning, but we already know.*

A moment of silence ensued. Susan turned from the cook stove, went to Billy, hugged and kissed him, and said, "I regret some of the things I said earlier. We'll go with you if you want us to. Mary Lynne's school starts again Monday, but we can tell her she's on a lark and maybe it won't last long."

Billy didn't thank Susan or allow a moment to pass before he asked, "How soon can you be ready?"

Susan did wait a moment, then said, "About a half hour. I have to pack for each of the children as well as for you and me."

"The next train east doesn't leave Fiskur for over an hour. Take that much time if you need it. I'll go out and watch the front and back of the house. We'll go by City Hall on our way to the train, and I'll leave a message there for the City Marshal to keep an eye on our house."

"You might be borrowing trouble again, but whatever you think."

They eventually boarded the train for the short trip to Humphrey, then went to a livery stable and hired a driver and buggy to take them to the Hastings house. They arrived before noon and found everybody all right, sort of, except they found Will in bed. Edith seemed a bit flustered by the presence of three children, and even more when she learned they intended to stay for a few days, but she found places for them all to sleep. Then Edith hurried to the kitchen to try to stretch their dinner. Susan played with the children so they wouldn't be underfoot, Billy took his .22 out of a gunny sack, and went outside. Susan came out on the porch after a while and yelled, "Dinner's ready."

Billy yelled back "Can you bring me a sandwich or a chicken leg or something to eat out here?"

Susan didn't answer, but went back inside. She returned soon with a plate of food and yelled "Where are you?"

"I'm up in this backyard tree."

"I have your dinner. Do you want to come down for it?"

"Yes. I see it. I'll just grab something I can take back up. I don't want to get surprised after we came all this way."

Susan shook her head. "You're borrowing trouble again, but whatever."

Billy waited all afternoon and saw nothing. He hoped he could stay awake all night. The moon didn't amount to much, snow didn't cover the ground, and darkness fell early. He nevertheless saw a match light a pipe among the trees behind the house, pointed his rifle in the approximate direction, and moved around behind the smallish tree trunk. When three figures stepped out from the trees toward the house, he yelled, "Stop. I can see you, but you can't see me. I can shoot you all before you take another step." The three figures moved back into the trees and he saw nothing the rest of the night or the next day. About midafternoon he went inside for a two hour nap, went back outside, and found a comfortable place to sit behind a tree in the front yard.

The second night also seemed darker than normal. Billy wanted to remain alert, but dozed early, and awoke with a start. One man may have gone in the front door of the house, but he saw two outside on the porch. He carefully moved around behind the tree and repeated his words of the night before. A man with a cane, one Billy recognized even in the dark, laughed out loud. He said, "You still tryin' to outsmart old Arch, Boy? When'll you ever learn?"

Billy almost panicked. He realized two, and probably three, criminals had gotten between his family and him. He decided to remain quiet and to hope the guys wouldn't know his location, would get nervous, and would leave. It didn't work. Arch jumped behind a porch post and fired his gun; Billy heard a bullet hit the tree opposite him. He didn't move out where Arch could see him, but spoke to Arch. "I'll come out, and I'll be your slave again, if you and your guys'll turn around and leave this house."

Arch responded, "That's a decent offer, Boy, but we got work to do here first. We got coal oil, and matches. This house, along with th' people in it—they're a gonna burn."

Billy stuck his rifle and his head around the tree, took as accurate an aim at Arch as he could in the darkness, and shot. He missed Arch, but hit the big fat guy behind him he surmised might be Zach. The fat guy fell with a thud, Arch turned to look, and Billy yelled,

"This next shot's for you, Arch. Drop that gun and move away from the house." He heard the back door slam.

Arch replied, "You're better'n I thought, boy, but Mort's right behind you. He's got the drop on you."

Billy didn't know the truthfulness of Arch's comment, but decided to be fearless and maybe stupid, and ignore it. "You're about to be dead, Arch, unless you walk—run, that is—away from the house."

Arch shot again. Billy answered in kind, Arch lifted his cane, and ran toward the road. Before he got there, a shorter person—maybe Mort—joined him. When they hit the road they turned toward Humphrey, and Billy watched them until he couldn't see them. He stepped over a dead person he recognized as Zach, and went inside to report.

Susan and Edith met Billy at the door. They each let out a sigh of relief. Susan said "Oh, Billy, I'm so glad to see you. One of those awful men came in here, went right to W.E., and we thought sure they'd killed you. He's the same guy who tried to take Robert years ago."

"Well, they did *try* to kill me. Ordinary men'd give up, but I don't know about those three—or two it is now. I went to sleep, or they wouldn't have got so close, and I wouldn't have had to shoot Zach. I feel terrible about Zach, and it's all because I couldn't stay awake. Jesus said to turn the other cheek, but nobody threatened His family. Still, I think He might have thought of another way. Maybe He'd just have stayed awake, and you better believe that's what I'll do the rest of the night."

Edith promised, "I'll go myself to git Sheriff Johnson. He can stop those guys."

Billy protested, "You can't do that Edith. They went toward Humphrey too. They might be hiding anyplace along the way, ready to jump out at you."

Edith responded, "Well, you can't stay awake day and night waiting for them. And one man against three—two—ain't a fair fight nohow. I'll go. I know another way to Humphrey, and I know where Sheriff Johnson lives. I'll start, jist as soon as I go out to the barn and saddle Clara, my horse."

Billy shook his head. "The whole idea makes no sense. But if you're determined, I'll go to the barn with you and make sure you're safe until you leave here."

"Do anything you want, but I'll go."

Edith went, and came back soon with Sheriff Johnson. The sheriff said he'd move Zach off the front porch, then bury him tomorrow, and watch the house the rest of the night. He said his deputy back in Humphrey sent word to the penitentiary people about the approximate locations of Arch and Mort, and he expected they'd catch them soon. Billy and Edith went back into the house; Billy crawled into bed with Susan, and Edith with Will. Billy quickly fell asleep, but woke up during the wee hours when he heard a gunshot. He grabbed his .22, peeked out the back door, and saw the sheriff put handcuffs on Arch and tie him to the tree behind the house—the one Billy had climbed. He continued to watch until the sheriff finished with Arch, and then quietly eased the door shut. He explained to Susan and went back to bed. Surely, he thought, Mort wouldn't come back alone.

The sheriff went back to Humphrey on Saturday morning, predicted somebody'd catch Mort before evening, but promised to come back about midnight to watch the house if Mort remained loose. Billy watched all day, and again nothing happened. That night, however, Mort came out of the trees behind the house, and Billy accosted him. Mort said, "Zach and Arch came here for revenge. I'm not that big on revenge, but you *didn't* treat me very nice when I came for your brother. You remember? I didn't get him then, but now you got a young boy of your own, and I intend to get that one."

"Mort, I threatened to shoot you once—it was mostly a bluff—but I'll do it this time, and it's not a bluff if I have to do it to protect any of my children from you. I have my rifle pointed at you right now. Do you understand that?"

"Yeah, I understand, and I'll go away for now, but I'll be back. You'll never know exactly when, but I'll be back. Count on it."

"What *you're* counting on, is that I won't shoot you now, to stop a later attack."

"Bye, Mr. Thomas." Mort stepped back into the darkness of the trees, and disappeared. Billy hoped the sheriff would return quickly, but didn't realize over two hours remained before midnight.

Billy went in Will and Edith's bedroom the next morning, told Edith and Will what had happened during the night, and then said, "I think I'm just the lightning rod bringing trouble down on you now. Arch is gone, and I think it's time for my family to go too."

Will answered, "You're prob'ly right, but we've felt safe all the time you been here. Edith and I thank you for that."

Billy then commented, "I think if my family goes, you'll continue to be safe. If Edith will take us to the train station today, we'll go back to Fiskur."

Edith took them to Humphrey in a wagon. During the short train ride to Fiskur, Billy sounded Susan out about the Knight farm. "What do you think about that?"

"I like the idea if you do."

"Sheriff Johnson said somebody'd probably catch Mort in a day or two, but we don't know for sure they will. If Mort goes to Fiskur, he'll probably look first at our house on Acorn Street. If we're out at the Knight place, it could take him a day or two more to find us, and give people more time to catch him. I'm tired of all the hassles and struggles we've been through almost all our married lives. I tried for years to be "fearless," as Mom once called me, but I think a lot of the time I'm just "stupid," as she also called me. The Knight farm'll be a lot of work, but maybe it'll be *just* work. I think you and the children will be safer out there."

"Whatever you think, Billy. I know you're looking out for the children, and I appreciate that. I look out for them too, and I couldn't agree more with your thinking. Even for smaller reasons, I'll be ecstatic if we move out there. I can't wait to have a garden, chickens, and get back to the life I grew up with."

"Fine. Let's go out to the Knights and hope we can move in today, to outfox old Mort, at least for a short time."

When they got off the train at Fiskur, Billy hired a buggy and driver to take them to the Knight farm. They arrived, and after some small talk, Billy asked Ron, "Is the offer you made earlier in the week still open?"

"Shore is."

"Susan and I've talked about it, and we'll take you up on it. Will the house and farm be available March 1?"

"You c'n have'em today. Gertie's got a uncle that's got a place out west, an' if we can use yore driver, we'll git on a train ta there as fast as we can, if that ain't too soon fer ya."

Billie looked at Susan, smiled, and replied, "That's perfect, Ron. Susan and the children will just stay, and I'll go back to Fiskur with you if you don't mind."

Gertie filled Susan and Billy in on the equipment and livestock they had. "Our farm's mostly creek bluff or good level upland fields, so Ron doesn't have a lot of livestock, but his team and equipment are first rate. As for livestock, we have twenty-one hens out in the barn, six more settin', four guinea hens, all with little ones, two turkey hens with little ones and a tom, twelve ewes due to lamb in March, and one sow, due to pig in about three weeks. He doesn't have a buck sheep or a boar hog because he borrows those from Old Man Chrushman ever' year. Crushman already came after them, so we don't have'em now. Because we have so little pasture, we don't have a milk cow—Ron goes down to the Haskellski house your mom used to live in ever' morning to buy milk. He runs the ewes in the timber on the bluff."

Billy went back to Fiskur and asked Ben Gibson to help him assemble the four people Ben said he had potential building contracts with. He asked and received permission to back out, then suggested, "Ben's a good builder. He might step in and do the work if you want to make contracts with him. What'cha say, Ben?"

Ben grimaced and replied, "I already have a job and don't want to quit it. Ben Jr. might do it after school and on Saturdays, but he'll take longer to do it than you would. Are you up for that, Junior?"

"I'm up for it if you'll help when you can and if you think I'm good enough."

"Great, Son. I'll help, and with all the practice you've had lately, you're good enough."

Ben and Ben Junior asked for the business Billy declined, and received that, plus another workshop! The meeting ended, Billy told the City Marshal about Mort's threat, and asked Sam to try to sell his house for him. He walked back out to the Knight place.

When he returned, he told Susan, "I think I can sleep for a week straight. I don't see how Mort can find us for at least a couple of days, so I'll sleep normally tonight and tomorrow night. The Marshal claims he can't do anything outside of Fiskur, but he did say he'd no-tify the sheriff in Riverbeach, so maybe we'll have some help. I hope nobody has to shoot Mort, especially me, but I won't let him at W.E. or either of the girls."

Susan grinned. "You've been under nothing but pressure lately. I'm glad you have a couple of days off, but what I'm mostly glad about is your fierce protective nature. Will said he felt safe around you. I want you to know, so do I. On another subject, Edith and I talked about a lot of things, including your condition when you got away from Arch. You didn't tell me all the worst details! And besides that, Edith thinks Will might not last through the winter. If he doesn't, don't you think we should go to his funeral?"

"Yeah, we should. And about Edith's talkative nature, she prob-ably remembers more than actually happened!"

Susan raised her right eyebrow, but didn't say anything.

CHAPTER TWELVE

The Farm

January 1914

BILLY AND HIS FAMILY went to the South Sinfe Church Sunday morning, January eleven. Susan and Billy expected to feel at home there but instead felt a bit like visitors. They enjoyed the time anyway, and told Pastor Javier they wanted to transfer their membership to South Sinfe.

The new Sheriff Glosshart visited the Thomas family on the farm on that same day, during the late afternoon. He said, "They caught Mort Callagher this mornin'. They're takin'im back to the state pen, so he'll be there with Arch Smith. They said they're gonna throw away the keys this time, and neither one o' 'em'll ever get out. "

"Thanks, Sheriff. That's uncommonly good news."

Billy went in the house. "Did you see that guy I talked to a minute ago?"

"Yes. Who is he?"

"He's the sheriff of Sinfe County. He said they caught Mort. That closes a chapter for us! I think I'll start my big forty-eight hour sleep right after supper tonight!"

During supper, however, they heard a knock on the door. Susan went. "Oh, hello, Pastor. Do come in."

Pastor Javier grinned, and replied, "All right, I will," as he stepped inside and took his hat off.

Susan smiled and asked, "What brings you here today, Pastor?"

The pastor turned toward Billy. "I want to perform a wedding in Riverbeach next Sunday, during our worship hour. If I do, I can't be in our church, so I came to ask you to tell what happened to you as part of the sermon then."

Billy all but jumped at the Pastor. "I'm no preacher. I can't do anything at all like that."

Pastor Javier took off his coat, sat on a chair, and appeared to settle in for a long evening. "That's why you'll be good. You might be nervous, but you'll be different, and people'll like that."

"No, I just can't do it."

"Nonsense. You know what happened to you, you're the true expert on that, and the only extra thing you have to do is tell about the faith that brought you through. Nobody except you knows about that either; people want to know and *need* to know. Your biggest problem'll be how to get it done in the time you have, but if you run over, don't worry about it. People won't want you to stop!"

Billy protested more, but eventually caved. Pastor Javier put his coat back on and left. Billy wondered why he agreed. He finished his supper and went to bed after a while, but though he remained tired, he couldn't sleep. The sermon nagged at his mind, and he tried to think of ways to either avoid it or to do it, instead of falling quickly asleep.

The next Sunday dawned clear and normally cold for early January, but the coal stove in the back of the church glowed cherry-red. Billy felt halfway ready, and mounted the platform to sit where Pastor Javier sat until time to preach. The song leader introduced him and he went to the pulpit. He told the terrible things he endured, and that Susan endured as well. People seemed riveted to his sermon, and even Mary Lynne sat still. Pastor Javier usually stopped at five minutes to twelve, but he hadn't yet gotten to the sermon part, so he continued— all the way to a quarter past noon, because he considered the sermon section the most important. He read his favorite scripture about loving God and about loving his neighbor as himself; next he read a passage from near the end of the Bible that said God rebukes those he loves; then he talked about the immense love God has for all people, the forgiveness he offers all people, and the perfect condition God will create in any person who allows it. He copied a phrase from Pastor Javier, and said, "in closing," then went on to note the symmetry of love—God loves us, he wants us to love Him; He expects everything from us, and He expects to do more for us than we can ever deserve or understand when we permit Him to do it.

It turned out Billy didn't really mean "in closing," because after the love talk, he said more; namely, "I didn't really think about God a lot while Arch had me or during my escape, but as I look back, I know God thought about me the whole time, loved me the whole time, and planned everything. I think the Arch episode was a rebuke from God— I can't say which of many possible reasons provoked Him, but I do know it's changed and improved me—it's made me less fearless and, as my mom would say, more "stupid," meaning more stupid in the world's eyes, or more subject to His guidance—and is more evidence of His love." Billy sat down, wiped sweat off his face, and semi-relaxed. The song leader prayed, then asked Billy to go to the back of the church and shake people's hands as they left.

Only about forty people heard the sermon, but many wanted to talk, to tell Billy his sermon moved them in a new way, and to tell him they'd pray for him. He shook hands and listened and talked for over an hour.

The outside temperature remained far below thirty-two degrees when Billy and his family eventually started home. They walked right past frosty grass and ice-covered ponds, and they talked. Susan hugged and kissed him before they left the church driveway, and told him what a great job he did. Approximately nine-year-old Mary Lynne hugged Susan first, then Billy, and told them she never before heard what they went through for her. Susan then jumped to a practical topic. "Let's walk fast. I left our dinner in the oven; the fire's burned down now, but still, I'm afraid it'll be burned."

Billy responded, "I can walk as fast as you can, and can carry Janet, but I'm not sure about W.E. I'm in a hurry too, not to see if dinner's burned, but to enjoy it, then to take another nap! You take W.E.'s hand and set the pace. I'll keep up."

"Whatever. Let me say again, you did a fabulous job today."

"It's a relief to have it over. If I ever seem about to say yes to Pastor Javier in the future, about anything whatever, slap me, will you?"

Susan giggled. "I will not! You preached a wonderful sermon, and I'd love to hear at least fifty-two of those every year!"

Billy frowned. "No chance. You'll never hear even one from me."

Out of breath W.E. entered the conversation. "Open your mouth, Dad. I want to see your teeth." Billy opened his mouth and looked at W.E.

Mary Lynne spoke next. "Take your shirt off, Mom, I want to see the scars Daddy talked about."

Susan answered, "Not here, Mary Lynne, but you've seen those scars every time you've watched me get ready for church or for anything else where I have to dress up."

"But Mom, I want to see them again. Dad, will you take your shirt off?"

Billy smiled. "Not even my coat! I might be like your mom. I'll do it at home after dinner, but not here."

"Mom, is Daddy not my real daddy?"

"Yes, Mary Lynne, he's your real daddy. He's W.E.'s and Janet's real daddy too. I'll tell you how and why when you're older."

"Will you tell W.E. and Janet too?"

"Yes, but you're the oldest, so I'll tell you first."

"Don't forget to show me your scars when we get home."

"I don't think I'll do it today, but you might ask Daddy."

"Daddy?"

"Yeah, I'll show you and W.E. too, after we get home, but you've both seen them a lot of times."

Mary Lynne laughed and then exclaimed, "Yay! We wanna see'em again!"

Billy brought up another subject before they arrived at the Knight house, their new home. "I'd like to buy our farm back from the Knights if they'll sell."

Susan frowned and glared. "I hope you don't want to move there. Nobody wants to live there except skunks and possums—I looked through the window Friday, so I know—they might like it, but I don't—and besides, it's too small for us."

"Well . . . I can clean it up and add another room. Or I could clean up the house after we buy it, and we could stay where we are. Then we could rent out only the house like I did once before."

"We don't have any money, Billy."

"How many people do you suppose buy farms out of savings these days?"

"Oh, Billy, you don't want to borrow money to buy a farm do you?"

"No, I don't want to, and we do need to buy a cow and fence off a pasture for her. That'll cost a little money. But I don't think it'll hurt to send a letter to Ron and ask what he wants for our old farm. It's only forty acres and he might let it go cheap. It hasn't been in his family for several generations or anything."

Susan continued to frown, but said, "I suppose it won't hurt to ask, just as long as we agree you're just asking, not getting committed to anything."

"Thanks, Susan. I'll write the letter today, let you read it, and re-write it if I have to, before I send it." Billy wrote a rough draft, and Susan almost blew up. "You want to buy *both* farms?"

"We already agreed it won't hurt to ask." He wrote again, and after several revisions, he and Susan agreed to send a short note: *What will you charge Susan and me for our old farm, and what for your original farm?*

Billy put the letter in the mailbox that evening, even though the mailman wouldn't come until after noon on Monday. The temperature already started to drop, and he went to the barn early to feed the various animals and to gather the eggs. Then he went back into the house for the evening.

Monday morning, after Billy fed the animals and ate breakfast, he took two milk bottles and walked down to the Haskellski house. He thought about the Knight house, his house, and Susan's aversion to his house as he walked down the hill toward Haskellski's. He walked the tree-lined Knight driveway and looked up. He saw the bare tree limbs joined and interlaced far above him and tried to imagine how it would look in summer, with leaves there. He thought about how the Knight house fit his family so well, with a ten by ten kitchen on the south, a ten by twelve sitting room adjacent to the kitchen, then a ten by twelve bedroom next, and a short hallway with ten by ten bedrooms on either side on the north, to form a T shape, and the openable windows on both sides of every room, to allow a cross breeze in summer. The kitchen even opened onto a small screened-in porch on the south with a second cook stove on it so Susan could cook in summer without heating up the whole house. The house also had a second heating stove at the far north end of the hallway—a sort of twin to the second cook stove. He decided he agreed with Susan they should stay put, but that made him think all the more they should buy the Knight farm too.

When he brought the milk back, he talked to Susan about the two farms. "I understand, Susan, why you want to stay in this house. I agree—it's better than the one down by the creek. But I think that means we want both farms."

"We can't afford both, Billy."

"Let's wait until Ron answers our letter. Maybe we can, especially if Sam sells our house in Fiskur."

"What if we can't? What if Sam doesn't sell the house?"

"Well, if we can't afford both, we'll buy only one. But we pay a sizeable rent on this house. That would end after two years if we owned it."

"What if we can't afford even one?"

"Well, then I suppose we don't buy any. Let's wait to hear from Ron before we decide."

"Whatever. Mary Lynne and I need to go now, to enroll her in Creekside Elementary/Secondary. We've been here a week already, and it's time we do that." Mary Lynne and Susan walked to the school in Joaquin County, on Monday, January twelve.

Billy walked down to the Haskellski house to buy milk, as he'd done during the previous week. This time, however, Mrs. Haskellski, a woman who reminded him of his mom, maybe not so much because she looked like his mom—she didn't, she stood a little taller with a younger, heavier frame, and had black hair—but perhaps because she lived in 'his mom's' house, asked a new question. "Do you want to buy my cow? Since Roger, my husband, died last year, it's been a chore for me to milk her. If you'll buy her, along with her little heifer calf, then I'll buy a quart of milk from you each day."

Billy grinned and answered, "Susan and I've been thinking we need to buy a cow. How much do you want?"

"I'll sell both for thirty dollars total. They might be worth a little more, but I really don't want to take care of them."

"I'll buy them if you'll keep them another week; I need to build some fence and Mary Lynne, W.E., and I'll come after her on Saturday afternoon, with thirty dollars total. I can also come down here twice every day and do the milking if I can take a quart a time home free. Will that work for you?"

"Oh would you do that? That will be perfect. I missed your sermon yesterday, by the way, and everybody tells me I missed a great one."

"I don't know about that last part, but yes, I'll do it. What's the cow's name?"

"Lizzy."

"Lizzy . . . thanks."

Billy took the milk home, and talked to Susan about Lizzy. Then he talked about where to build the fence. "You know, as I walked past our former farm, it occurred to me we should keep Lizzy down there. I think I'll move the chickens down there too. But back to Lizzy, there're already *two* two acre enclosures down there. The wire's pretty loose and a cow could walk through it in a few places, but I think the posts are all right, and a couple of new strands of barbed wire ought to fix everything up fine. The barn roof's more of a worry to me than the fence, though. I think I can go into Fiskur for a few bundles of shingles and patch it to last a year or two, but it's gonna need a whole new roof before long."

"Billy, we haven't heard from Ron yet, and you already think the farm is ours?"

"It's ours to own or to rent. And except for a bottomland field along the creek, it's more of a grass farm than a crop farm. It doesn't matter whether we own the two farms or rent them, we should use each in the best way, don't you think?"

"Well, maybe. Just don't plan to own that farm again. We do need a cow, but we don't have the money to buy a farm."

"Yes, Dear." Billy walked away. He went down to look at the barn roof again, both from the front side and from the back side, and to decide how many bundles of shingles he needed to fix it.

He came back before noon, and after dinner, said, "I think I'll hitch Ron's horses to his wagon tomorrow, and go into Fiskur. I could cut the big cedar tree in the yard down the hill, and then try to split shingles out of it, but it's the only decent-sized cedar we have, and I can get better shingles a lot faster from Clark and Sharp."

"Whatever you think, Dear. Just don't let 'farm purchase' get stuck in your head!"

Billy went out Tuesday morning, went to Fiskur and back, and unloaded four bundles of shingles and three rolls of barbed wire by the barn at his former farm. Then he ate a late lunch and did his evening chores, which included milking Lizzy at Mrs. Haskellski's place.

After he finished his morning chores and took milk back home on Wednesday, he patched the barn roof, so he could milk Lizzy in it and stay dry during rain, and so he could move Ron's chickens into it. He checked his pocket watch when he finished, and realized he needed to get down from the roof as fast as he could, and he almost ran up the hill to get home in time for the noon meal Susan had ready.

He took a nap after lunch, then went out to the mail box. He hoped to find a letter from Ron, but didn't, so he went down the hill and patched the 'Lizzy fences.' He did his evening chores and went inside for supper. After supper, he went into Ron's barn, plucked seven hens off their roost, and took them down the hill to their new home. He had to make two more trips; he decided to leave the 'setting' hens alone until they raised their chicks. He took the turkey hens on one trip, and carried the turkey chicks in two buckets on a final trip. The guineas roosted outside, and he ignored them. He planned to catch them later as needed for the table, and to not replace them after they were gone.

Billy came back inside and talked to W.E. and Mary Lynne after he did all that and before they went to bed. "I told Mrs. Haskellski we'd buy her cow on Saturday, but I don't think she'll mind if we're a few days early. I want you to hurry home Mary Lynne—don't run, but don't dilly-dally—tomorrow after school, and you and W.E. can help me move Lizzy from her old home to her new one down the hill. I'll expect you about . . . half past four."

Mary Lynne came home a couple minutes earlier than Billy expected; they both went down the hill with W.E. and thirty dollars. Billy went all the way to Mrs. Haskellski's house, told W.E. to wait in the Knight driveway to turn Lizzy south toward 'their' barn, and told Mary Lynne to wait in the road just past 'their' driveway, and turn Lizzy and her calf into it, toward the barn, when she came that way. After Lizzy and the calf went in the barn, Billy allowed W.E. and Mary Lynne to go on home. He milked Lizzy, penned the calf in the barn, and put Lizzy back out into one of the two-acre pastures.

The remainder of January didn't seem unusual, except for three problems. Billy showed Mary Lynne how to gather the eggs, but the very first day she went alone, she came back soon and ran into the house. Her little dress had dirt on the front, her face had more dirt with tear-cleaned stripes, and her chin and nose dripped blood. She wailed, "Daddy's gonna spank me, Daddy's gonna spank me."

Susan first grabbed a washcloth, then hugged Mary Lynne, and asked, "Why would Daddy spank you?"

After another series of "Daddy's gonna spank me's," Mary Lynne calmed enough to also say, among cries, "Mr. Tom wouldn't let me go in with the chickens."

"Is that what why you're crying?"

"Yes . . . Daddy's gonna spank me."

Susan caused Mary Lynne to cry more when she asked, "How'd you get so dirty?"

When Mary Lynne could crowd words among her sobs again, she said, "I fell . . . down in . . . the barn lot."

"Is that how you skinned your face, too?"

"Yes . . . I fell down in the barn lot. Daddy's gonna spank me."

"No, Mary Lynne, Daddy won't spank you because Mr. Tom's a bad boy. Come on, I'll go back with you, just as soon as we get some dirt off your face."

Mary Lynne cried more, and even screamed, not only because she didn't want her face wiped, but also because she didn't want to go back near Mr. Tom. She tried to explain. "We can't go there, Momma. Mr. Tom will eat us both, and then Daddy will spank us both."

"Daddy won't spank anybody because of what Mr. Tom did." Susan took Mary Lynne's hand and pulled her to the barn entrance. 'Mr. Tom' met them there, and scared both of them away. Susan said, "Daddy won't be scared. Let's go back in the house and let him take care of Mr. Tom."

"Daddy's gonna spank both of us."

"No, Mary Lynne. If anybody gets in trouble, it'll be 'Mr. Tom.'"

Mary Lynne didn't calm down until Billy came in the house. Susan told him the story, and he went back outside. He returned with the eggs and said, "I didn't see the turkey, but Mary Lynne, how will you feel about gathering eggs tomorrow if we have turkey for dinner first?"

"I don't ever wanna go back to the barn. The little turkeys might grow big like Mr. Tom."

"I'll go with you until you feel all right about it."

"Mommy said you won't spank me?"

"Of course not. You went, you tried, and you didn't do anything wrong."

"Can we pray for Mr. Tom before we eat him?"

"We definitely can. We can do it right now, or at dinnertime. You pick."

"Let's do it now."

"You want to go first, or me?"

"I don't want to do it. You."

"All right, but I want to pray for some people too, if I do it."

"You do it."

"All right. *Dear God, please be with Mr. Tom, and take his soul (if he has one) to be with you. Also, be with Mr. Little, Arch Smith, and Mort Callagher. Help them to feel your fabulous love, and to realize you'll make them perfect if they let you do it. Finally, please be with Mary Lynne, W.E., Janet Sue, me, Mom, and all people on the earth. Help us all to realize the same thing. Amen.*

Susan cooked Mr. Tom for dinner on Sunday. On Monday and Tuesday, Billy went with Mary Lynne to gather eggs, and they had no more trouble. Then she agreed with Billy she could do it alone. She named herself the best egg gatherer in two counties before the winter ended.

Billy also worried about dry weather. November had some rain, but he thought they went into December a bit on the dry side, and December had little snow or rain. January had none. All the farmers at South Sinfe Church worried about the dry winter, as did Billy. He didn't want to sell any of Ron's ewes. Although they continued to forage in the woods, and he expected the spring to be all right, he worried about summer and fall. Ron had a small amount of sheep-quality hay in his barn, plus plenty of oats and corn. Lizzy could eat stockpiled grass outside, but Billy brought her some corn from Ron's barn at each milking, and planned to add the cost of it to his February 1 house rent.

He looked in the mail box each day for an answer to his letter about the cost to buy back 'his' farm, but nothing came until Wednesday, January 28. The body of the letter read: *I only paid $200 for your place, and I'll let it go back to you for that. My place, also 40 acres, might be worth as much as $1400, but I know you'll take care of it, and I'll sell it to you (only) for a even $1000. That includes the buildins, the stock, and the equipment. Your payin $40 rent on the house ever month, and if you send $200 for the old Thomas place, and double your rent, you can pay off the farm in a little over two years. (We're countin on the rent for the next couple of years, whether you do or don't buy the farm.) Or if you skip the extry part ever other month, it will take near five. However you want to pay, we want to sell, and will take payment as you can do it, for however long it takes.*

I apologize for the delay, but we live up in the Wyomin mountins, and the mailman don't come ever day.

Billy read the letter before he returned to the house from the mailbox. He gave the letter to Susan and waited. She said, "Well, it doesn't look as bad as I expected. I still think we're better off with money than with two farms."

"Let's talk about them one at a time. We have enough we can pay for our place today. I say we do it."

"Maybe that one, but how could we send the money? The post office warns against sending money in a letter."

"We mailed a letter on Monday with a money order in it. We could go back to the bank and buy one for $200 tomorrow."

"Don't you think that's a little quick?"

"If we're gonna do it, why wait?"

"It might be the right thing, Billy, but I just worry about us not having hardly any savings left. What if one of the children gets sick?"

"I know you worry about us not having a reserve, Susan, but we *will* have. We'll have the farm we can borrow against, and Sam'll sell our house one of these days. Then we'll have cash under the bed again."

"It goes against every instinct I have, but if we can stay here, I trust your judgment."

"You already know I once said I'd rather move back into 'our' house, but if we buy this one, we'll have to pay rent on it anyway for two years, and then we'll have two houses. I still might fix up the other one to rent out for a little extra cash. If we *don't* buy this farm, we'll have to pay rent on the house as long as our agreement continues with the Knights."

"Should I understand that to say you want to buy *both* farms?"

"I think everything I said's true, if we do or don't, but you know I do want to buy both."

"Well, again, Billy, we don't have the money."

"Ron said we can pay as we get it. I should write back tomorrow, and I want to accept both his offers. Is that all right with you?"

"It's dumb, Billy, but again, if you want to take on that obligation, I'll join you in it."

"Thanks, Susan."

Billy wrote a letter to Gertie and Ron, showed it to Susan, and mailed it on Thursday from the post office after he went to the bank for a money order to put in it. The letter said: *We want to buy both farms. You made us two very good offers and we can't pass them up! We already paid our house rent for February, plus some extra for corn as I already explained. This letter has payment for the Thomas place, and we plan to begin to pay for your place with our next house rent payment.*

Billy no longer worried about having to sell Ron's sheep after they bought the Knight farm, with livestock. Instead, he worried about having to sell *his* sheep. He hoped for warmer and wetter weather in February, and thought rain and snow closer to normal, but the ground remained frozen and much of the February moisture ran off. February daytime temperature highs ran mostly above freezing, sometimes well above, but the nighttime lows remained low, often far below thirty-two degrees. He did recognize a bright spot, however. The corn and hay in Ron's barn became his corn and his hay in his barn.

He hoped for a warm, early March, with drier weather at the end so he could sow oats near the end of March. He judged early March perhaps only slightly warmer than normal, but he didn't see even one snowflake or drop of rain. Late March featured a mild wet spell, and even though he wanted to sow oats, he welcomed the rain. He intended to sow oats on the Thomas place, but it remained wet, so he changed his plan and sowed oats on a drier field on the Knight place on Saturday, April four. Rain returned on the sixth with well over an inch, but except for a couple little sprinkles and a barely larger amount, no more fell in April. Pastures Billy expected to be lush and almost ready to cut for hay, weren't. He put a temporary fence across the middle of his oat field and turned the sheep into it. The field didn't have a pond, so he had to drive them to water twice a day.

He planted one field of corn into dry dirt on Monday, May four, had to stop on Tuesday because of a small shower, but resumed on Wednesday, and finished on the following Monday, with no more rain to stop his planting and no significant rain during the remainder of the month.

About an inch of rain fell on June first and second, so he replanted corn on Thursday, June 4 into moist dirt. Rainfall remained sparse through August, and temperatures climbed over a hundred degrees a few times in July, but Billy realized at the end of August, the summer could have been worse. He cut a little oat hay, left a few acres for grain, and moved the sheep back to the woods during June. The oat hay and oat grain yielded well, and even the corn silked and filled following the few rains that fell, and Billy predicted at least twenty-five bushels of corn per acre, about average for the area. Another bright spot in August happened when Mary Lynne won a youth club sewing contest, and got her picture in both the *Fiskur Democrat* and the *Kansas City Times*.

The skies opened up during the first full week of September, and Billy thought that a third bright spot. He talked with Susan about it at dinner on Saturday, September 12. "I think these good rains will put water in the subsoil and will break the drought."

Susan grew up a farmer's daughter, and knew the importance of weather to farmers. But she thought Billy had an unhealthy obsession with it. "I hope you're right. When you worked for somebody else, you didn't care at all about the weather, and even when you had a building business, if it rained, you just waited until it ended, then went back to work." She put on a mischievous grin to tell Billy her following words meant nothing. "Maybe you ought to look for a job with Clark and Sharp in Fiskur, or with a hardware store there. Sam still hasn't sold our house, so we could merely move back into it."

Billy grinned back. "Or maybe I could just work for Arch again, and let him bear all the risk."

Mary Lynne cried, then pleaded, "Please don't leave us, Daddy. Don't go back to Arch."

Billy started to speak, but Susan beat him to it. "Oh, honey, Daddy's just being silly. He'd never, ever, leave us, and would never go back to Arch. Arch's in jail anyway. You know that."

Billy added, "Yes, Mary Lynne, Mommy's right. You know all that."

"Yes, I know all that, but I don't want you to even say it."

Billy agreed again, "All right, Mary Lynne, if you don't want me to say it, I won't, ever again."

Mary Lynne giggled, they continued their dinner, and Billy went back out to look at crops again.

CHAPTER THIRTEEN

Big and Harvey T. Little

September 1914

THE THIRD PROBLEM OCCURRED early the following Monday evening. Billy, W.E., and Mary Lynne went to the Thomas barn to milk the cow and gather the eggs. They finished, came out of the barn, and Billy heard Susan scream from all the way up the hill and in the house. He stood rooted in place for a moment, then Susan screamed again. He started to run up the hill, yelled back over his shoulder to W.E. and Mary Lynne to stay, and ran at his top speed, as Susan continued to scream. He ran to the two front porch steps, took them in one jump, pulled the porch screen door screws completely out of the wood as he jerked the door open, and ran, out of breath, into the kitchen. He saw Susan in a chair there, as an average-size, well dressed man in a top hat and white gloves stood near her. Susan saw Billy and screamed even louder than before. Billy'd never seen the man, but jumped between Susan and the man, and pushed him toward the kitchen door. The man gave ground easily, stumbled, but righted himself and grabbed the kitchen door jambs with his hands. Billy followed and pushed once more. The man almost fell out onto the porch, but stumbled to the opening to the outside, and held to the edges of it. Billy's third push caused him to fall down the two steps and onto his back. He rolled sideways, got away from Billy's pounce, ran, and mounted a mostly white mare. Billy had failed to notice the mare as he ran toward the house, but thought he should have. He chased the man and the mare a short distance, until the mare whirled, and knocked Billy against a nearby woodpile. He grabbed at the man, but caught only air.

The man kicked the mare and seemed about to go down the driveway and get away, when Mary Lynne jogged into the front yard, ahead of W.E. The man put out his left arm as if to pull Mary Lynne up with him. Mary Lynne reached up toward the place the man's hand would soon be. Billy grabbed a stick of cook wood and threw it at the man. He missed the man badly, and instead hit the mare on the upper left rear leg. She bucked one time, up in back and to the right. The man fell off over the mare's head, she turned around with her nose close to the man, and stood there. When the man fell off, he rolled again, but before Billy jumped, and into his jump. Billy pinned the man on his back, with arms to his sides. He marveled at how little the man resisted, but lowered his face near the man's and growled, "Who are you? Why are you here?"

The man didn't answer. Mary Lynne came near, and Billy said, "Go in the house and find out if this blockhead hurt Mother." She went, W.E. arrived, and Billy told him to go inside too. Before he could go in, Susan came and stood in the gap at the edge of the porch where the door had been.

She temporarily replaced her screams with sobs, but when she saw the man under Billy, she screamed, "That's Big Little," and continued to cry.

Billy suddenly understood her terror, and asked, "Did he hurt you?"

Susan managed a "No," between sobs.

Billy again spoke to the man. "You don't know how lucky you are you didn't hurt her. I'll send my boy across the road to get a rope out of the barn to tie you, and the next person you can try to scare'll be the Joaquin County Sheriff."

The man answered this time. "The little girl's my daughter. I saw her picture in the paper, and I live in the nicest house in south Kansas City. I can give her a good life. Just let me up."

"Your daughter, eh? You gonna give her the same good life you gave her mother?"

"I never touched her mother. That was my brother Harvey."

"You never touched her? How can you call the girl your daughter?"

"She's my goddaughter."

"Yeah, right. That's not the way her mother tells it."

"The girl's mother is a lying, no good—"

"That's not the Susan I know. Perhaps you talk about yourself."

"Just let me up and let me take my daughter."

Their talk started quietly, but gradually became louder, so Susan could hear.

She screamed again, "He'll take her over my dead body!"

Billy didn't loosen his grip on Big Little, but talked to Susan again. "Keep Mary Lynne in the house and send W.E. across the road to get the rope off the second horse stall wall."

Big Little lapsed into a sullen silence and didn't talk more. W.E. arrived with the rope, Billy rolled the man over, and tied his hands behind his back. He said to W.E., "We'll take this man to Jaker to see the sheriff. We can all three ride his horse," but Susan screamed again, and yelled, "Don't leave Mary Lynne and me here alone. Little Little might show up any minute."

Billy looked at W.E. again., and spoke loudly enough for Susan to hear. "I know you've never done this Son, but can you get the horses in the barn? I'll tie the man's feet with whatever I can find; then I'll come out and harness the horses, hitch up the wagon, and we can all go to Jaker." He turned to Susan and yelled, "Do you have a tea towel I can use to tie Big with?"

He tied Big Little's feet and loaded him into the wagon, along with Susan and the children, but they barely started down the driveway when a bullet from behind went into the dirt beside them. Billy pushed Susan and the three children down into the wagon box, followed them, and yelled, "Hey! Come out where I can see you." He cowered in the wagon box and couldn't have seen anyone unless that someone looked over the edge. He heard another bullet and didn't know where it went, but concluded the person either didn't know how to shoot or didn't want to shoot them. He jumped over the edge of the wagon immediately after the second shot and ran to hide behind a nearby tree, but didn't hear another shot. After a while he yelled again. "Who are you?"

A juvenile voice answered, "I'm Ida Little, Mrs. Oscar Little, Oscar's wife. I hate him but it's my duty to protect him."

Billy replied, "I could tell you stuff about the man I bet you don't know, but for right now, come on down here; we'll take you to Jaker too."

A young girl, barely older than Mary Lynne, came out from behind a front yard tree, with a gun pointed approximately at the wagon. The girl trembled and shook.

Billy called, "Drop the pistol, girl, and we won't hurt you." She dropped it and walked, crying, toward the wagon.

Billy jumped out and grabbed the girl's arm when she neared the wagon. He asked, "If we don't tie you up, will you ride quietly, and not try to jump out or to untie . . . Oscar?"

She couldn't speak because she cried too much, but she nodded yes. Billy noticed some teeth out, still bloody wounds on her face, and bandages on her arms. He wondered, "How long you been married to that clown . . . Oscar?"

She could barely answer, owing to her tears. "I'm not sure, but I am. His brother performed the ceremony himself, right in Oscar's house."

"Will you tell the sheriff about anything bad you've endured at Oscar's hands?"

"Are you positive he won't get away and take me back? What about the brothers?" They reached the wagon, and Susan began to nod yes.

Billy said, "I won't let him get away. I can't speak for the sheriff, but if you tell him all you know, I can't imagine he will either."

"I don't know. I sure don't want to go back, and if he gets loose, he'll take me. And I'm afraid of the brothers."

Billy already knew about Harvey, and worried about him too. He didn't really want an extra twelve- to fifteen- year-old child, but offered, "You can stay with Susan and me for a few years if you like. I'll make either of the Littles skidoo if they come around here."

Susan spoke. "Come on girl, get in the wagon. I know a lot about this guy too. Together we can put him away for the rest of his life. And there's no better protector than Billy." Ida climbed into the wagon and crowded onto the spring seat with Billy and Susan. The three children moved to the back of the wagon, and Billy started down the hill again.

They made it halfway to the bridge at the bottom of the drive-way when a short skinny man Susan later identified as Harvey Little popped out from the trees along the edge of the driveway. He wore clothes similar to Oscar's, including white gloves, and pointed a gun at Ida. He ordered, "Untie Oscar, then get out of the wagon and stand behind me."

Billy first thought she'd do it, and wondered if she'd be a reli-able ally even if she didn't. She hesitated, seemed reluctant to obey, and Billy caught her eye. He did an almost imperceptible no shake of his head. Ida set her jaw, opened her mouth to reply to Harvey, but Su-san put a mystified look on her face and asked, "Oscar? Who's Oscar?" Harvey answered, "I saw what you did to him, and I'm here to undo it. Now untie him."

Susan spoke again. "That's bunk, you goopy louse. You better drop that doodad you point at Ida, because if you don't, Billy'll clean your plow in a way you might not survive."

Harvey echoed Billy's sentiment. "How'll that hillbilly clean anybody's plow while I have a gun on Ida?"

Ida then spoke. "You're gonna go to the pokey, Harvey. I don't know this man, but he can push your face in the dirt with one hand behind his back. He has Oscar tied in back, he has a lot of allies up front in the wagon, and in back too. You're about to see how unless you drop that gun."

Ida's first words seemed to signal Mary Lynne and W.E. to leave the wagon, because they both jumped out the back. Harvey shot under the wagon into the dirt, and the horses reared and jumped backward a step. Mary Lynne and W.E. ran to opposite sides of the road and disappeared behind the trees just as Harvey shot again at W.E. Susan gasped and stood. Harvey repointed the gun at her, and said, "Stay in the wagon. You leave, you're dead." Susan continued to stand, but stayed in the wagon.

Mary Lynne first, then W.E. also, appeared in the driveway close to the bridge, behind Harvey. Susan yelled, "Hide in the woods, children." Harvey turned to give a quick glance back. Billy jumped out of the wagon, stood so one of the horses partly shielded him, and charged Harvey when he looked back again. Susan jumped off the other side of the wagon the second time Harvey looked back. He looked at Susan again and tried to move his gun to follow her, but Billy ran into him and knocked him flat on his back almost instantly. Harvey went down easily, hit his head on a rock, and seemed disoriented and groggy for several seconds.

Ida jumped off the wagon, stood over the almost out Harvey, and yelled, "That's how. You're gonna go to the pokey, hooray, and I'll be free. I'm free now, and you can't get me back into that fancy house of yours."

Harvey revived, felt his head and said, "Huh?"

Billy told Harvey to get in the wagon and to lie next to Oscar. He did. Billy then told Susan to point Harvey's pistol at him and to shoot him if he moved. Susan grinned, then said, "If the wagon bounces, my trigger finger might do a fatal wiggle!"

Billy quickly said, "You can't do that, Susan. Do you think Mary Lynne ought to hold the pistol?"

Susan assured, "Oh, Billy, I was only joking. I can do it." She switched topics. "It looks like Mary Lynne will miss school today, but so be it. I won't leave her here by herself."

The group went to Jaker, and arrived in the night. They found a tall, sad-eyed, young and lanky Deputy Sheriff, Luke Hazelton, who told them Sheriff Jim Everly went home about five o'clock. Susan, Ida, and Billy told Luke everything they knew about Harvey and Oscar. Susan's and Ida's stories turned out to be similar, and Billy told of his experience with Oscar and Harvey earlier in the afternoon. Luke looked distraught. He said, "I think I need to send for the sheriff. He should hear this; can you wait and tell him all about it?"

Susan answered, "Absolutely. I've lived in fear of these two for years. I'll do anything humanly possible to know I'm safe from them." They waited for the sheriff, and Luke locked the Littles in a cell together. They didn't start home until near midnight. They talked about sleeping alongside the road somewhere, but Susan said she hadn't even shut the door to the house when they left, Janet Sue could sleep in her arms, and she thought they should get back.

As they rode back home in the wagon, soon after they left Jaker, Susan erupted. "I hate those guys. I wish you'd killed them, Billy."

Ida voiced the same opinion, but Billy countered, "Jesus said we should love our enemies. He didn't say to try to shield them from punishment, but he also didn't say to kill them. He loves them. I admit I didn't love them when they threatened us, but I'm ready to try now. I hope you are too." He looked first at Susan and then at Ida. They both looked skeptical, but said they'd try.

Later in the trip, Billy talked on a different subject. "I invited you to stay with us, Ida. You'll need to sleep for a while when we get home, but what do you plan after tomorrow?"

"I appreciate you asking, but I have parents over in Olathe—that's in Kansas. I want to see them again, and I think they'll protect me if those two monsters—or loveable monsters the way you talk about them—ever get out of jail. The thing I don't know is how I'll get there. And two more things; please think of me as Ida Smithson, not Ida Little. Susan makes me think I'm not really married to Oscar, and I hope I'm not."

Billy allowed a short silence, then said, "I agree. You're probably not married. Don't worry about how to get to Olathe. I know we'll think of something. I'll think on it tonight. But what's the second thing?"

"I'm so sleepy and so scared I don't even want to talk about it tonight. Can we do it tomorrow?"

Billy said, "Sure." They arrived home in time to see faint glimmers of light on the eastern horizon. They crashed, and didn't awaken until nearly noon.

During their breakfast, as they called it, Billy asked, "Do you know where Olathe is, Ida? I've never heard of it, so I don't."

"Sort of. I could get there, but I'd have to go to Oscar's place in Kansas City first, then go from there. I don't want to go near Oscar's place again though, even if I think he's in Jaker. I'd be scared of him and of his brothers."

"You won't have to go by yourself. We'll all go with you—or maybe just me. Mary Lynne's already missed two days of school and doesn't need to miss more." Billy looked at Susan. "Will you and the children feel safe here for several days without me? W.E. and Mary Lynne can do the chores except for milking Lizzy, and maybe I can persuade Mrs. Haskellski to do that part."

"Oh yes, we feel safe, now that those terrible Littles are locked up—we're safer than we've been since . . . since Boston."

Billy looked back to Ida. "I'll see Mrs. Haskellski today; if she can't milk Lizzy for some reason, I'll put the calf out with her. And we can leave early tomorrow. I think we can ride double on Oscar's mare. Do you know how far out Olathe is into Kansas?" When Ida assured Billy it was barely over the state line, he continued. "Maybe we can leave at first light, push the mare, and get there in one day. Then I can take two days to come back, and go easy on the mare on the return."

Ida asked, "Aren't you afraid of the brother?"

Billy looked perplexed and answered, "They're both locked in a cell in Jaker."

"Don't you know about the third one?"

Susan looked perplexed this time, and responded, "The third one?"

"Yeah, the big one, the retarded one."

Billy said, "We only know about two. Did a third one hurt you in Kansas City?"

"Only once. I don't think he lives with the other two, but he's meaner'n a big cootie."

Billy asked, "Is that the second thing you talked about last night?"

"Yes."

"Did this third brother know where Harvey and Oscar found us?"

"I don't know. He's not terribly bright."

Billy talked to Susan. "A third brother might change things. Do you still feel safe?

Susan looked at the floor, then at Billy. "Maybe not. Maybe the guy doesn't know where his brothers went. But maybe he does. Would you wait here just a few days before you go? If he's coming for us, he'll probably come soon."

"Yeah, sure, Susan. Or we can all go if you want. I can find somebody to take care of the animals while we're gone, but it might take longer than just this afternoon."

"I really don't want to go, but I don't want to be alone here with the children, either."

"It might take an extra day, but we can all go in the wagon."

"I'm sick of the wagon. It makes my side hurt. Can you rent a buggy? Maybe the children and I can stay here, if you'll wait to go until next week."

"We can rent a buggy or wait several weeks—if Ida will stand for it. I do think somebody should go with her when she goes."

"If the third brother comes, he'll surely do it before next week. I'll be nervous until you get back, but it could be best if you and Ida go alone on Monday."

Billy and Ida left early Monday morning, before they could see well. They first went to South Kansas City, approached the Little house, and Billy suggested they detour a couple blocks around it, just in case. He told Ida, "My mom always said I'm fearless and stupid, and I'm beginning to think the two go togeher! It might border on stupid to ride down the street past Little's."

Ida instantly agreed, they detoured, and went on to Olathe. Billy dropped Ida off, met her parents, and accepted their gratitude. He resisted their invitation to stay the night, and left after only a few minutes. He knew he couldn't account for Ida's wounds, and didn't want to try. He also didn't want to leave Susan alone a second longer than necessary. The sun set before they arrived at Ida's, but Billy found more direct roads toward home than the roads they traveled during the day; he rode for about two more hours and made good progress. Then he slept under a tree beside the road and set out again early the next morning. He trotted the mare part of the time, and arrived home Tuesday, in the late afternoon.

Susan greeted him with kisses, hugs, and words. "Oh Billy, I feel so free. I've worried the Littles might find me since Boston. Now I have reason to hope they'll be in jail years and years and years. Maybe the third brother doesn't know or care about me. I hope he doesn't, anyway."

"You might have to testify at a trial. Are you willing to see Oscar and Harvey again?"

"Yes, if it means they're gone from my life. What about Ida? Will they want her to testify?"

"Probably, if they want you, but I know her address to give a lawyer if he wants to know."

"You're so great, Billy. I always feel safe when you're around, and you always protect me! I love you so much!"

Billy basked, but eventually asked, "Where are the children?"

"Janet 's asleep in the back bedroom. Two others went down to the Thomas barn to play in the hay, and the fourth is in here." She pointed at her belly.

Billy grinned big. "You mean . . . "

"Yeah, that's what I mean."

"I intended to spend some time outside today, but you've changed my mind—I'm gonna stay in the rest of the day. When do you figure it'll come?"

"I don't know for sure, maybe around March or April."

Neither Billy nor Susan accomplished any useful work the remainder of the day.

CHAPTER FOURTEEN

The Baby
March 1915

THE END OF FEBRUARY WEATHER had been decently mild, as had the beginning of March. But Susan didn't feel well, had stayed indoors most of February, and had even acted irritated by the children. Billy tried to take care of the fires and the children as much as he could, and although he couldn't stay in the house all the time, he spent most of most days there. Susan talked to him about baby names. She asked if he liked dozens of names, but eventually settled on June Lee if a girl and Robert Lee if a boy.

She awakened Billy before dawn on March 11, and told him "I think the baby's coming today. Maybe you ought to go after Marge Haskellski."

"I'll go, but you know she thinks you should have Dr. Chisholm instead."

"Oh, what does Marge know? Just get her, and if she still thinks she wants Dr. Chisholm, and if I agree, then maybe."

Billy walked fast down to the Haskellski house, listened to Marge's harangue about a doctor as they walked back, and they went into the quiet house. They found Susan drenched in sweat, moaning incoherently, and seemingly unconscious. Marge looked worried and triumphant at the same time. She said, "Told you."

Billy ran back outside, hunted in the dark for Oskena, as he called Oscar's mare, found her after several minutes, saddled her, and galloped off to Dr. Chisholm's house in Fiskur. Dr. Chisholm seemed so slow that Billy returned ahead of him, and arrived several minutes before the doctor. He slid off Oskena, didn't tie her, and ran inside. Susan didn't talk to Billy, but Marge did. "You bring the doctor?"

"He's on the way."

"He'd better hurry. If he doesn't, we'll lose either Susan or the baby, if not both."

"No! Is there anything I can do?"

"Yes—go outside and wait."

"I can't do that. Anything else?"

"No. Just go outside, away from here."

"Maybe I'll go back and meet Dr. Chisholm and tell him to hurry."

"Good."

Billy went out, found Oskena grazing in the front yard, jumped on, and started back to Fiskur. He met Dr. Chisholm on the driveway in his buggy, impeccably dressed in a white shirt, tie, black trousers, and black shoes. He yelled, "Hurry. Marge thinks Susan might not be alive much longer."

"Keep your shirt on, Boy. I'll get there when I get there."

"Please make it sooner, rather than later!"

Dr. Chisholm didn't reply, but Billy thought he seemed unduly careful and slow as he tied his horse to a tree, before he ambled into the house. Billy tried to follow, but Dr. Chisholm stood in the doorway and said, "Wait here, Boy. I'll bring your baby out for you to see when it's here."

Billy waited. After an hour or so, Dr. Chisholm came back to the doorway. He looked harried, had blood on his shirt, and announced, "We saved Susan, but couldn't save the baby."

Billy didn't hesitate. He said, "Out of my way, Doc. I'm comin' in." He swatted at Dr. Chisholm, went into the bedroom, and saw a wan and feeble Susan. He grabbed her hand and asked, "How do you feel?"

Marge answered. "She doesn't feel good. She doesn't feel like talking. Go away and leave her alone."

Susan protested, "No, stay. We don't have to talk, but stay."

Billy stayed until the doctor left. He called after Dr. Chisholm when he left, "I'll be in later today to settle up, Doc."

Marge shook her head, shrugged, went into the kitchen and made breakfast, including hot tea for Susan. Billy thanked her for coming and for her thoughtfulness, then she went home, with the three children in tow.

As soon as Marge left, Susan started to cry.

Billy squeezed Susan's hand, and said, "I'm sorry."

"For what?"

"That Robert didn't pull through."

Susan cried more, and didn't answer. Billy held her hand until almost noon, then said, "I should go make dinner for us. Anything you want?"

She stopped crying, and tried to grin. "Nothing we have. Whatever you make'll be fine."

Billy went to the kitchen, and realized he couldn't cook. He found some bread and butter, plus some grape jelly, and brought that to Susan. She only ate one slice of bread with butter and jelly, but praised him for it, and then asked about the children.

Billy answered, "They went home with Marge. Should I go after them?"

"Maybe after a bit. I don't hurt anywhere, but I don't even want to move yet."

"Sure, Susan. They're fine with Marge, and I'll go when you say, but even then I'll keep them out of your room as long as you want. I might have to be out with them."

Billy held Susan's hand until near evening, then she claimed to feel strong enough to cook supper, and asked Billy to go after the children. He built up the fire in the cook stove and went. They came back to find supper on the kitchen table, but Susan in a chair in the next room. She said she felt better, but wasn't hungry. Billy played with the children after supper, put them to bed, helped Susan to bed, and greeted her the next morning. "How do you feel today?"

"So much better you wouldn't believe it. I might challenge you to a footrace after breakfast!" Billy watched for signs of weakness for a few days, but didn't see them.

He forgot about payment due Dr. Chisholm the day before, but went that day. He asked Dr. Chisholm, "You think Susan'll be all right?"

"Yeah, sure, why wouldn't she be?"

"Can she have more children?"

"How old is she?"

"Thirty-three."

"She probably won't have more anyway."

"But can she?"

"Maybe. I wouldn't worry too much about yesterday. These things happen."

Susan recovered enough to walk to Robert's funeral at South Sinfe Church Saturday, and then to ride in the wagon to Humphrey to Will's funeral the Tuesday after. She seemed shattered emotionally both times, but suffered no physical after-effects.

Much later, in May of that year, she talked about Robert more. "Billy, I don't understand how I can love a boy I never saw alive, but I love Robert fully as much as I love our other children. How can that be?"

"I don't know, Susan, but it might be normal. I think it would be wrong for either of us to just forget about him. You want to go for a walk this afternoon, pick some flowers, and put them on his grave?"

"I'd like that, Billy." They took the walk that day, and other days.

⬥

CHAPTER FIFTEEN

The Trial, the House, the Barn, the War and the Knights

1915

BILLY THOUGHT THE FARM PROFITABLE by mid May of 1915. He had two cows down at the Thomas farm, a good renter in the house there, 39 ewes he kept on the Knight farm bluff part of the time and on the Thomas farm part of the time, he had a decent harvest in 1914, he expected to pay off the Knight farm in about a year, and his growing oats and corn, though small, looked good. A sheriff's deputy knocked on their door about noon on Monday, May 24. He asked for Susan, gave her a paper, and asked her to sign it. She asked, "What's this?"

"It's a summons. The two Littles go on trial Monday of next week, and Judge Clemons wants you there in case a lawyer calls you to testify. Do you know where I can find Miss Ida Smithson?"

"Billy does. Can you tell the deputy where she is, Billy?"

Billy went to the door and answered, "She lived at 2323 South Orange Trail in Olathe, the last I knew."

The deputy looked skeptical. "I thought she lived in South Kansas City."

Billy shook his head no. "The Littles enslaved her there, but she hasn't lived there since you locked-em up—the Littles."

"Well, either way I won't make it tonight. I guess I'll have to go back to Jaker."

Susan invited, "You can stay here tonight if you like. Supper'll be part of the deal, and we're about to sit down if you want that too."

"Naw, I don't have any money. I'll just go on back."

Susan tried again. "You don't need money. It's on the house."

"Naw, I need to tell people where I'm at anyhow, so I might as well go on back . . . I would eat supper before I go, if that much of your offer's still open."

The deputy, not Luke Hazleton, but shorter, stockier, and named Jim Ryder, ate supper with them. He left, and they saw him again at the trial, along with Ida, her dad, and the Little twins. Ida no longer had bandages on her arms, but had scars there, and on her face. With their scars and their teeth out, Susan and Ida looked almost like mother and daughter; Billy thought their mere presence enough to convict the Littles. He shook hands with Ida's dad, with Sheriff Everhart, and both deputies. Ida's dad told Billy he didn't know Ida's location or the extent of her problem until she told him after Billy brought her home.

They went to the new courthouse in Jaker the next Monday. They went up some stairs and entered the courtroom through a door in the south wall. They walked past an empty judge's chair on their right, but could see a man in a judge's robe in a small, book-lined room beyond. They walked past a rail on their left with jurors behind it, around the back of a long, painted, curved seat, like a church pew, centered on a spot behind the judge's chair. The curved seat they walked past was last in a set of four. They sat on the far end of that last curved seat, next to a small room labeled 'Jury Room,' on the east side of the bigger room. Harvey and Oscar sat at one of two little dark brown tables in front of the curved seats, along with a third man they supposed might be a lawyer. A fourth man sat at the other little table. They saw writing pads, pencils, and books on the tables.

Susan and Ida didn't participate much in the trial, and only had to go back one more day, but Oscar repeatedly twisted in his seat and mouthed death threats to them on that Monday. Harvey, on the other hand, ignored them, ignored Oscar, and seemed a perfect gentleman.

Neither Susan nor Ida testified Monday, but the judge told them to be back on Tuesday. Susan invited the Smithsons to stay with them Monday night. They found a livery stable in Jaker, left their buggy and horse there, and rode to the farm in Billy and Susan's wagon. All the children, including Ida, sat at the back of the wagon, and the adults sat on the spring seat in front. Susan talked to Mr. Smithson, Ira, during the entire trip. "I can't get over how *young* Ida acts. She giggles and plays with Mary Lynne now, but last year, she seemed older, sadder, like an old lady."

Ira smiled, then answered. "Yes, she had a tough time with the Littles, but she's learning to be a little girl again. She's only thirteen, you know."

"Really! Our Mary Lynne isn't far behind. She's eleven, about to be twelve."

Ira didn't act interested in Mary Lynne, but returned to his talk about Ida. "She had nightmares every night for a while, so we took her to Topeka for a long vacation. She still wakes us sometimes with her nightmares, but less often."

"Really? I had them too, and still have them, but rarely. They may never stop."

"Ida told us how you and your family rescued her. We can't thank you enough."

"We're glad we helped, but I think Billy tried more to rescue me, than Ida!"

They continued with mostly small talk the remainder of the trip.

Susan and Ida both testified on Tuesday. The man they'd first seen at the second table called them as witnesses and told them to show the gaps in their teeth. He also told them to hold up their arms, to turn slowly around with their blouses pulled up a few inches, and to describe other injuries they couldn't show. Finally, he had them tell about their nightmares, and the so-called 'wedding ceremonies.' The man also seemed interested in Mary Lynne, her adoption, and how Susan could know her father was Harvey. Billy hoped she wouldn't talk too much and jeopardize the adoption. She didn't, but also didn't answer all the lawyer's questions.

The man from the first table cross-examined them, but in a cursory way. Billy said he was probably appointed by the court and got paid, even for a minor effort. He thought he should be called to testify also, but it didn't happen.

He went to Fiskur every day after the trial, to buy a copy of the *Jaker Star Journal* newspaper. The paper said the trial ended on Thursday, June third. The jury found both twins guilty of kidnapping, assault, and impersonating clergymen. They would be sentenced the next day.

The Friday paper said Harvey and Oscar were both sentenced to twenty years in the state penitentiary at Jefferson City. Susan read the sentence, yelled out a "Yipee!" and continued, "I'm thirty-four now, and in twenty years I'll be fifty-four. Maybe the Littles won't want me at that age . . . and with any luck, Ida'll be married, will have a different name, and a husband to protect her. In any case, maybe some law officer somewhere will keep an eye on them. I hope their kidnapping career is over!"

Billy grinned and threatened, "I'll be fifty-five, and my arthritic shoulder, the one the wagon ran over, might not work then, but if I have one arm and can walk, they'd better not come around here!"

A couple weeks later, on a Saturday in June, Sam Mesker came out to say he'd sold their house and lot in Fiskur, for $2,500, three hundred more than Billy and Susan told him they wanted. Billy ignored Sam for a short time when he heard the amount. "Wow, Susan, we can pay off the $580 we owe Ron, we can keep the $40 times . . . 7 we still owe him for rent, we can give a double tithe to South Sinfe Church, and still have over a thousand to save!" He then turned to Sam. "Thanks a ton, Sam. I'd like to offer you a hundred dollars for selling the house. Who bought it?"

Sam and Susan both started to speak, but Sam prevailed. "I might take fifty, but a hundred is way too much. The buyer is Ben Junior, Ben Gibson's boy—he's to be married Sunday to a neighbor girl named Lois. I felt guilty asking so much, but he didn't quibble, he just pulled the cash money out of his pocket, twenty-five brand new hundred dollar bills."

Susan jumped into the conversation when Sam stopped. "A thousand dollars to save sounds good, Billy, but do you think we ought to wait a bit on the tithe and on the farm payoff?"

Billy said, "Just a second, Susan. We can talk about that later." He and Sam then argued about the fifty or hundred, Sam eventually accepted the one hundred dollar bill Billy waved in his face, and went back to Fiskur. Billy then asked Susan to repeat, and she did.

Billy responded. "We have less than a hundred savings now. I'll think we're in great shape if we up it by more than ten-fold—how much do you think we need?"

"I don't know, Billy, but just because we have money isn't, by itself, a good reason to spend it."

Mary Lynne and W.E. stood behind Billy and Susan. Mary Lynne interrupted, "I want new shoes and a new dress I don't have to make out of a feed sack."

W.E. added, "And I want new shoes too."

Susan acknowledged the needs, but rebutted Billy. "You see? Once we start to spend, we can't stop."

"I don't think any of that's too much. We'll still be able to save over a thousand. Who needs more'n that?"

"Well, maybe I'm all right with paying off debt, and even shoes and a dress, but a *double* tithe? Where'd that notion come from?"

"That's another form of saving, Susan. Except not for us."

"Don't you ever worry about us?"

"Yes, Susan, but not about money for us . . . especially not now. Do you realize we've added to our livestock without spending, our crops look good, and we don't need the house money at all? The thing I worry about isn't money, it's Tim Bolivan and people like him. What if he comes out here to gripe about us selling our house to Ben Junior? What if I'm not inside when—if—he comes?"

Mary Lynne asked, "Who's Tim Bolivan?"

Susan answered, "He's a bad man, Mary Lynne, but don't worry about him at all. Daddy's just borrowing trouble again."

Billy spoke. "I hope you're right. But about the tithe—Sam already got most of it for us, above what we expected."

"But Billy, you just gave a hundred of it back to Sam."

Billy shrugged. "Whatever you think. You decide if you think five hundred's too much to tithe. You already know what I think."

They let the subject drop, and didn't discuss it again until after the next Sunday, on Saturday, July third. Billy asked, "Did you decide anything about a tithe yet?"

Susan said with a frown, "Whatever you think, Billy. I can do without if you can."

"Great, Susan. Why don't you take the money and drop it into the plate yourself?"

"Whatever." She took the money to South Sinfe the next day, and that discussion ended, but not for long, because less than a week later, on July 6, lightning struck the Thomas barn and it burned to the ground. Billy had two calves and some chickens in the barn and got them out, but lost all the hay inside (a lot), and all the grain (not much). He caught the chickens that night and moved them to the Knight barn, built an outdoor stanchion and an outdoor pen for the calves during the next three days, then built the barn back during the following two months, but Susan mentioned the tithe again.

"Do you think the barn burned because God thinks we should have saved more money to rebuild it?"

"I don't think so, Susan, do you?"

"How can I know what God thinks? I know what I think, though, and I think we should have."

"We didn't need more than a few dollars, Susan. Our neighbors helped me cut logs, haul them to the sawmill, haul the lumber back, and build the barn. The biggest money expenses were shingles, door and gate hinges, and paint. You probably remember a couple things the

Bible says about tithes. I know I do, because I looked them up last week. *Bring ye all the tithes . . . and prove me now herewith, saith the Lord of hosts, if I will not open you the windows of heaven and pour you out a blessing that there shall not be room enough to receive it.* And *Honour the Lord with thy substance, and with the firstfruits of all thine increase: So shall thy barns be filled with plenty . . .* You remember those?"

"I've read them, but they don't work, Billy. We paid the tithe *before* the barn burned, remember?"

"Yes, we did, but do you remember the song we sang in church a few Sundays back, something about how God moves in mysterious ways His wonders to perform?"

"I don't want to argue about it any more, Billy. We donated the tithe, our barn burned, and we had a loss. That's all I know. Let's drop the subject." They did, for a longer time than before.

Other problems cropped up during the summer of 1915 and later. Because a war started in Europe and spread to involve the U.S., Billy eventually received a letter from a draft board in Jaker. He replied with a letter, but the draft board wrote a second letter to tell him that as a farmer and as the support for his family, he'd be exempted. He didn't want to leave Susan and the children, and accepted the exemption.

Billy and Susan received three more letters that summer: one from Gertie Knight, who wrote Ron had something called leukemia and didn't feel bad, but didn't expect to live more than a few months. She also wrote that he wanted to die at home, and asked if they could come back for a few weeks.

Billy asked, "Do you know exactly what Gertie wants? Does she want to be a guest, or does she want the farm back?"

"I don't know, but if she wants the farm back, we can't give it to her, can we?"

"Maybe that isn't what she wants. Can you write a letter back, invite them to stay as guests, and hope she'll leave it that way?"

"Are you sure I shouldn't be more plain-spoken? I don't see 'hope' as a substantial thing."

"I favor doing it the other way, and we can get 'plain-spoken' later, if we have to."

"That's all right with me, if you'll do it."

"I might do it, but we don't have to decide today, do we?"

Susan sighed. "I'll do it your way, but I think it means we've already decided."

A couple days after the Knight letter, one came from Kitty in Strick. It said Robert and Ed were to be married at ten am, August tenth, in a double ceremony, and that Tim and a girl named Alice seemed to be serious. She invited Billy and Susan to come for the double, and possibly another later.

Susan knew Billy would want to go, but said, "The timing's awful. We don't know when the Knights will come, and we almost have to be here when they're here. I want to go. Robert and Ed are like brothers to me too, but I think we should wait to decide until we know when the Knights plan to come, and we might have to decide not to go."

"You might be right, Susan. But if we wait too long to accept, Kitty might interpret the delay as a no. I think we need to answer inside of a week. Maybe the Knights will answer your letter that fast. You did send it didn't you?"

"I sent it. If we show up, we're there, regardless of how Kitty interprets anything."

"Maybe."

The Knights wrote back to say they'd arrive during the week of August twenty-three, so Susan wrote Kitty they'd arrive at Huntington, West Virginia at five pm on the eighth, and someone would need to pick them up there. But on the fifth, Ben Wilson rode up the driveway and knocked on the door. He asked Billy if he remembered his comment that he'd help Ben if he needed it later. Billy remembered. Ben told a sad story about his wife, Sally, and her recent affliction with dementia. He wondered if Susan could come and take care of her, maybe as much as every other week for a year or more. Susan overheard. She tried to control the negative look on her face and invited Ben inside for iced tea, a cookie, and a rest. Ben tried to say no, but Susan insisted. She put Ben in a chair in the sitting room, and summoned Billy to the kitchen.

She asked, "Do you think Mary Lynne's old enough to go, part time? She's somewhere around twelve now."

"I don't know, Susan. She wants to go to Strick with us, pretty bad."

"Well, either Mary Lynne stays home from Strick, or I do."

"Wow. I know you both want to go."

"Yes—wait, I gotta take tea in to Ben." She took the tea, and came back.

"Ben helped me when no one else would. If it wasn't for Ben, we'd likely have never found each other again."

"I know, Billy. You have to decide. Do you want me to go with you, or do you want Mary Lynne to go?"

"Can you just go in there and say yes to Ben, then we decide later how we'll make good? We both owe Ben big time."

"That's dumb, Billy. How can we promise if we don't know how we'll do it?"

"It might be dumb, but we gotta say something, probably within the next half a minute. And I want to say yes."

"All right, Billy, but it's still dumb."

It turned out Mary Lynne almost looked forward to getting away from home, but didn't want to miss the wedding. In the end, Susan persuaded Marge Haskellski to go to Ben's for five days, Susan and Mary Lynne went together through August seventh, so Mary Lynne could see what she would have to do after they came back from Strick, and how to do it. They wrote Kitty again to postpone their arrival to the ninth. They did arrive on the ninth, but not until after eleven pm. A washed-out bridge in Ohio stopped their train for over an hour in Indiana, then they had to make a detour and stop at every little town along the way. Billy complained to Susan about it. "This train doesn't even go through Ohio. Why can't we just go on as we planned?"

"I don't know, Billy. Maybe it has to do with other trains. You think we'll miss the wedding?"

"The conductor said we'd get to Huntington on the right date, just late at night. We're on the train—we can't go back, so I guess we have to tough it out. The part I don't know how to handle is how to get from Huntington to Strick. Tim said he'd be there at five, but he probably gave up and went home a long time before now."

They got off the train at Huntington, about twenty minutes later than the second promise, and saw Tim waiting. After the grown-ups hugged and greeted, Billy said, "Wow, Tim. You must have wondered if we'd make it."

Tim grinned, and explained, "The agent inside said you'd be late. He even predicted your arrival time and got sort of close!"

Susan said, "Maybe we ought to just go to Kitty's place. All three of the children are asleep, and I don't want to wake them if we can help it."

"Tim grinned again. "Yeah, sure, Susan. If we can get them in the buggy asleep, then we can get to Strick in about an hour. I'll run the horse part of the time. Have you-all met Alice, my girl friend?"

Susan seemed more awake than Billy, and she answered, "No! We haven't! Kitty mentioned her, and we do want to meet her. Hi, Alice." Susan extended her left hand, because she held Mary Lynne in her right.

Alice, about a head shorter than average-height Tim, looked dressed up, but in cheap clothes. She also appeared painfully shy— she answered Susan's short greeting with an even shorter reply, "Hi," and seemed confused by Susan's left hand. She eventually shook it with her left.

Tim and Susan talked along the way. She asked, "Do you still live in Kitty's house?"

"Yeah. I'll be by myself there after tomorrow, but Kitty says I can stay." He frowned slightly and continued. "She says if I ever have Alice over, I have to notify her at least twenty-four hours ahead, so she can send Cindy Lou over as a chaperone. I may move out over that issue."

Susan grinned. "Perhaps you should listen to your Aunt Kitty. It sounds like she knows you better than you know yourself!"

"Maybe, but I don't think so. I'm twenty-three years old for crying out loud, and Alice is a year and a half older than me."

Susan didn't answer for a moment. Then she asked, "Where do you work now?"

"I work five days a week as a waiter at Louie's Restaurant in downtown Strick, but I make almost as much money on Saturdays, at Clyde Evans Hardware, where Billy used to work."

"Do people ever talk about Billy there?"

"Not much. They talk more about Robert and Ed. They worked there after Billy did."

"When they talk about Billy, what kinds of things do they say?"

"Mostly, it's just about how they do something—they say Billy did it that way and they never changed it—usually it has to do with records or money handling. Sometimes they use Billy, or Robert, or Ed as time markers. They might say such and such happened about a year, or two, or whatever, after one of the two left."

They found Robert and Ed already asleep when they arrived at Kitty's house, and wasted no time afterward making pallets and falling asleep. Cindy Lou woke them the next morning about seven, to say Kitty asked her to make breakfast for them, and they could come now. Everybody, including Mary Lynne and W.E., talked faster at breakfast than they ate.

The wedding went well. Twenty-six-year-old Robert and twenty-four-year-old Ed looked muscular and handsome in matching new dark blue suits with white shirts and blue ties. The brides, possibly a little younger, also wore matching gowns with matching bouquets. Robert's bride, Samantha, shorter than Robert, with black hair and a perfect figure, walked up the aisle beside Ed's Opal, about the same height as Ed, also with black hair, and maybe a mite thin. The ceremony lasted almost an hour, and Billy with his family had to get back to Huntington in time to catch a twelve forty-eight train, so the visits at breakfast time turned out to be all they had. Billy did most of the talking with Tim on the way back to Huntington. He said, "I wish we didn't have to get back so soon, but I know Robert and Ed have better things to do today than talk to us anyway!"

Tim grinned. "Yeah, probably."

"Tell them we're sorry we got here so late, and didn't do more than briefly meet their new wives."

"Will do."

"Do you and Alice plan to marry soon?"

"We've talked about it—right Alice?—but I'm looking at a new job driving mules and a wagon to Louisville and back, and don't expect to be home much. So we've decided to wait a few years." Billy processed that information for a moment, and Tim continued, "The last time you were here, people in Fiskur wanted your scalp. Has that settled down any?"

"Yeah, some. Actually, a lot. What do you think about Tim's work plans, Alice?"

Alice blushed and stammered, but didn't say intelligible words. So Tim answered, "She's on board."

They made small talk most of the trip, got to Huntington just in time to catch their train, and Billy thought they didn't even have time to properly say goodbye to Tim. They got on the train, and Billy said to Susan, "Well, I'm disappointed. We made a long trip, spent hours on a train, and didn't even get to talk much to anybody."

Mary Lynne added, "Yes, I thought Uncle Ed had a daughter about my age I could play with. He doesn't."

Susan grinned and started to answer, but W.E. interrupted her. "He doesn't have a boy either. I wish I'd stayed home."

Susan answered them both. "How could Uncle Ed have a son or daughter when he didn't get married until today?"

Almost two-year-old Janet Sue chimed in. "I don't care how. I just want kids to play with."

174

Billy admonished, "We'll need to write a thank you note to Kitty, and when we do, we don't want to grouse about kids." Mary Lynne seemed about to speak, so Billy hurried to ask her, "Are you all set to go take care of Mrs. Wilson when we get back?"

"I thought Mommy would do it first."

"I don't know. Is that right, Susan?"

"Yes, that's right."

"Maybe I ought to go up for a two or three day stint, too."

Susan responded instantly. "You can't do that, Billy. Sally uses a bedpan, she needs a bath every day, and she'd be most uncomfortable with you. She's not all there, but she's enough there to know you're not the right person."

"Then maybe I ought to go up there to spell Ben on chores for a few days. I think I ought to do something. We both have a big debt to pay Ben."

Susan grinned. "Now *that's* a good idea, Billy. Why don't you wait until I come back on Sunday, then go with Mary Lynne for her three days?"

"If you think that'll work, I'll do it. I'll put calves with the cows and you and W.E. can feed, gather the eggs and so on."

W.E. looked pained. "It's Mary Lynne's job to do all that stuff."

Billy put his arm across W.E.'s shoulders and answered, "Mary Lynne won't be home because she'll be helping Mrs. Wilson. That leaves you as the big guy in the house. I'll count on you to do whatever Mommy says to do." He winked at W.E. and grinned at Susan. "She's not a bad boss, you know."

W.E. continued to look pained, but didn't answer. The long train ride ended on Tuesday, they said hello to Sam, and walked all the way home. Susan and Mary Lynne alternated in three day sets, with one night at home for them both, between sets. Both Mary Lynne and Susan rode Oskena to and from Sally's house. Susan interrupted the three-day sets she and Mary Lynne spent at the Wilsons, to be back from Sally's about six the evening of Wednesday, August twenty-fifth, so both she and Mary Lynne would be home all night after the Knight's arrived in a chauffeured buggy before noon that day. Mary Lynne cooked dinner Thursday, and Billy commended her for a great job.

Neither Gertie nor Ron said anything about taking the farm back, but seemed grateful to merely be there. Ron looked feeble and sick by then, and though he could walk around in the house and come to meals, he spent much time in bed.

Susan went out to the barn to talk to Billy one day when Mary Lynne helped Sally. She explained everything to Billy, and asked, "Can you go to the Wilsons and ask Mary Lynne to stay indefinitely? I don't think I can leave here."

"I think you should talk to Gertie, then go relieve Mary Lynne. She and I can entertain the Knights as well as you can. And anyway, Gertie's here to take care of Ron, not to be entertained."

They argued more, but Susan went to the Wilson house, Mary Lynne came home, and cooked and cleaned like a grown-up. She went back one more time, but she didn't go back more times, because school started in September. Billy asked Marge Haskellski to take Mary Lynne's place for a while and she agreed to do it. Ron died, Tuesday, September 9, 1915. He was buried Thursday in the South Sinfe Church cemetery, and Billy felt almost as bad as he did when they buried Robert there.

Gertie seemed in no hurry to go back to Wyoming, and after a few days suggested she go take care of Sally Wilson. She said she'd gone to school with Sally years before, and thought caring for her a service she could perform, and it provided a place for her to live for a while. Billy thought Gertie's plan a good one, and rode double on Oskena to get her there. He talked to Ben while at his house. "Ben, I'd like to come here and do your chores on Monday through Wednesday, every week. You need a break, and that's something I can do."

Ben responded with a tired little smile, and with not much effort to say no. After only a brief resistance, he agreed.

Billy spoke again. "It isn't Monday, but I'll do two and a half days this week, starting today, if you'll show me what to do this evening. I'll look around in your barn while I'm there and see if anything needs repair. If it does, I'll bring stuff to fix it with when I come back on Monday." He found only a couple broken boards on a corncrib wall. He removed them the next day, then replaced them with two good boards from the top of the crib. He put the broken boards at the top, and thought breaks wouldn't matter up there anyway.

Shortly after Gertie went to the Wilsons house, Susan invited Mary Lynne to go for a walk, just the two of them. When they cleared the front yard, Susan asked, "Do you remember when you asked if Daddy's your real daddy, and I said I'd talk to you about it when you were older?"

"No."

"Well, it happened, and I intended to wait a few more years, but you've been so . . . mature lately, I think it's time now."

They continued to walk, and Susan seemed lost in thought, so Mary Lynne asked, "Yes?"

"I told you Daddy's your real daddy, and that's true. It's been true since he adopted you when you were only about two years old. But you had a different daddy before that, the Harvey Little we took to Jaker. You know all about Harvey, and that he's a bad man?"

"Will I be bad like him?"

"Oh no, Mary Lynne. I don't think you will. I love you too much, Daddy loves you too much, and Jesus loves you too much. Even if you turn out to be awful, you won't be able to get rid of our love! And I know you won't ever be awful, because Daddy and I pray for you every day."

"Where did Daddy come from?"

"He and I were married long before you were born."

"Did Daddy adopt W.E. and Janet Sue?"

"No, they were born after Daddy came back to me."

"Where did he go?"

"You know. You know all about Arch."

"I love you, Mommy. I wanted to know all that."

"I love you too. And so does Daddy and so does Jesus."

"And that's why I won't be bad?"

"That's why you never need to even worry about being bad. We're almost to South Sinfe Church. You want to look for flowers to put on Robert's and Ron's graves?"

They found flowers, and turned toward home after they deposited them. Susan thought they had a worthwhile conversation. Mary Lynne ran on ahead to tell W.E. where they went.

CHAPTER SIXTEEN

The Burning Cross

October 1915

BILLY LOOKED AT HIS CORN FIELDS on a Monday in October. They looked good, and he planned to sweep out the nearly empty corn cribs in both barns the next day, to make them ready for new corn. He didn't sweep the next day, because a small group of hooded and sheeted people came to his front yard that night and burned a cross there. That's all they did, and Billy didn't feel undue alarm, but decided to go to Fiskur the next day to confront Tim Bolivan. Even though the apparent leader of the cross-burning group wore a hood and sheet Billy felt sure he was Tim—both because of his previous behavior and because the person looked so small.

Billy saddled Oskena on Tuesday morning, and rode to Elmer's Drug in Fiskur, where he knew Tim worked. Tim set a Cherry Phosphate on the fountain counter for a customer just as Billy arrived. He didn't try to keep his voice down as he said, "Did you think you scared anybody last night?"

Tim wiped his pale face with his hand, looked uncomfortable, and answered, "What'a you mean?"

Billy said, "Don't worry about it, Tim. I'm too busy and too tired to make anything out of it. Just don't do it again."

Ted permitted a nervous grin, and asked again, "What'a you mean?"

Billy looked over his shoulder as he went back outside. "I mean don't do it again." He stopped by Ben Jr.'s house on the way home, but nobody answered the door. So he went back to the train station to tell Sam to warn Ben Jr. to be careful, then went on home.

He pulled the remnant of the cross out of the shallow hole the burners dug for the base of it when he got home, stored it in the upper barn, and walked down the driveway to find a place to stand behind a tree near the bridge.

After supper that night, Billy waited behind the tree he found earlier in the day. He didn't bother to take his .22 with him. He saw a small bunch of riders carrying flaming torches turn off the road about two am. He waited until the little man at the head of the group reached the bridge, then stepped in front of them and spoke to the little guy. "Tim, I told you yesterday I'm too busy for this stuff. Turn around and go back to Fiskur. If your little mind needs to stir up trouble, stir it up closer to home."

The small man answered, "You sold your house to a black boy, and that's not acceptable. You're gonna hafta pay."

"That 'boy' can use you to mop all of Fiskur. Be sure you don't parade around by his house in your fancy get-up, or he might do it."

"You're the guy should be scared."

"Do you think I'm less likely to harm you than Ben, Jr. is?"

"I don't like your attitude."

"Do I look like I care? Turn around and go on home before I have to spank you."

The little person turned to look at the people behind him, but couldn't see their faces because of the hoods. One at the back, however, pointed toward the road, turned his horse, and rode that way. The others followed, leaving the little one alone until he also turned his horse and followed, at the rear of the group.

Billy watched them until even the small guy reached the road and turned toward Fiskur. Then he also turned, and walked up the driveway. He looked again when he reached the top, and could see no one. He went on inside and went to bed.

The next morning at breakfast, Susan asked what happened. Billy said, "Nothing. Tim and his guys knew they were wrong, so they left."

W.E. didn't believe it could be that easy. "How many of'em did you shoot, Dad?"

"None, W.E. They turned around after only a real little argument."

W.E. continued. "But Dad, you could have shot'em easy."

Billy smiled. "And what would have happened next, Son?"

Mary Lynne raised her hand and jumped up and down in her chair as she would do at school. Billy asked, "What is it Mary Lynne?"

Mary Lynne assumed a knowing look and answered, "They'd fall down."

W.E. nodded, but Billy replied, "Yeah, they'd fall down, but the next night there'd be more, and the sheriff'd be out here— to shoot somebody would make the uproar worse and make it last longer."

Susan worried, "It could last longer anyway, you know."

Billy smiled with more confidence than he really had. "Maybe, but I don't think so." He returned to his regular work after breakfast, swept out the bins he'd planned to clean the day before, mended a broken place on a harness, and did a few other odd jobs.

Early in the evening, after the children went to bed but before he and Susan did, she heard a scratching noise on the east side of the house. She looked out the window, gasped, and screeched, "Come over here, Billy, and look." He went to the window, saw some dead tree limbs piled against the house, and saw the little hooded guy he felt sure he recognized as Tim Bolivan, dragging more toward it. He looked for more people, but didn't see any.

Billy acted unruffled, and said, "It's Tim again. I'll go out and run him off."

Susan blocked the doorway to the kitchen. "No, let's take the children out a west window and run. Let him have the house, but I won't let him harm the children."

"Susan, it's only Tim. I can still use both arms, but only need about a half of one to cow him."

"How do you know he's alone?"

"If he wasn't, we'd see more people. Get out of the doorway. I need to go before he torches that woodpile out there." Billy gestured toward the east.

"At least take your rifle."

Billy grinned. "I won't need it." Then he sobered. "But I do need to get out there now." He crowded past Susan, stormed through the kitchen and out onto the front porch. Eight to ten men, all in sheets and hoods, filled the side edges of the porch. Billy's first running step took him to the middle of the crowd, where someone pinned his arms in a bear hug.

Tim came to the porch door holding a rope. "Looks like operation decoy worked. See that tree limb up there, Billy? You're about to hang from it."

A rifle barrel, plus Susan's right side, appeared in the kitchen door between it and the porch. Susan yelled, "I can't shoot you, Tim, because you're hiding behind Billy. But I can shoot any of these other guys, and I'll kill one dead if Billy's not back in here in two seconds." The bear hug guy loosened his grip and pushed Billy back toward the kitchen. Tim pulled a pistol and shot part of Billy's left ear off. The bullet went on to hit the top of Susan's right hand and come out the bottom. It went from her hand to make a furrow in the floor behind her.

Billy saw what happened to Susan, charged Tim, and nearly tackled him before he shot again and hit him in the upper chest. Billy fell and one of the sheeted men on the porch said, "Let's get out of here." Almost as one, the men ran out the door, ran over and trampled on Tim, continued to run all the way to the driveway and part way down it. They untied their horses there, jumped on them, and galloped on down the driveway.

Tim didn't seem to realize he'd incapacitated both Billy and Susan, because he struggled to his feet and hobbled after the others. He didn't bother to untie his horse, but followed the others on foot.

All the noise awoke Mary Lynne and W.E. They came from their bedrooms and encountered Susan, who said to Mary Lynne, "You go out past the barn, then turn toward Marge Haskellski's, but stay in the trees and off the road. Tell Marge to get up here, also in the trees and off the road, as fast as she can. And W.E., you go through the woods to the next road west and tell Mr. Crushman to go for Dr. Chisholm, *now*. Go, both of you."

Mary Lynne asked, "What happened to your hand?"

Susan yelled, "Just go!"

Mary Lynne started out the kitchen door, but stopped when she saw Billy lying on the porch. Susan screamed at both W.E. and Mary Lynne, "Go now!"

They went, and Susan looked at Billy's motionless back. She saw no blood and no hole in his shirt. She turned him over on his back, and saw a small hole in his shirt. She also saw a big flow of blood out the hole but saw no evidence he remained conscious. She ripped his shirt open with her left hand and stuffed a corner of a tea towel into the hole in his chest. Then she talked to him.

"Billy, just hang on, please, please hang on. W.E.'s gone for Dr. Chisholm." She paused a moment, and asked, "Billy, can you hear me?" She continued to urge him to stay alive until Marge and Mary Lynne arrived.

Marge ordered Mary Lynne to go back to bed, but she answered, "That's my dad. I'll stay here."

Marge ordered her again, but Susan said, "Let her stay. It won't be easy for her, but she wouldn't sleep in bed. The important thing is to stop Billy's bleeding. I tried, but didn't do a good job."

"Mary Lynne said you've been shot too. Let me see."

Susan put her right hand behind her back. "It hurts, but I'll live. Billy might not—pay attention to him."

Marge gripped Billy's shoulder to turn him again, but Susan stopped her. "I've looked. The bullet is still inside."

"Then we're gonna need Dr. Chisholm to get it out."

"W.E. already went to send Jim Crushman to bring the doctor."

"Then why am I here?"

"I need somebody here, and Billy needs you here to stop the bleeding."

"Honey, I'm here for you, but I don't know if I can do much more about the bleeding than you've done."

"Billy's the priority. Do what you can."

W.E. came back and said, "Mr. Crushman left on a horse." He stared at Billy and started to cry. Before Susan could comfort him, he asked, "Is Daddy dead?"

"No, W.E., he's gonna be all right. Just stand over there by Mary Lynne, out of Marge's way, and we'll wait for Dr. Chisholm." W.E. went to join the crying Mary Lynne standing against the west porch wall. He cried more, and Susan did as well.

Everybody, including Marge, stood around, cried, and waited for Dr. Chisholm. He arrived with Jim Crushman after about two hours, set his bag on a chair on the porch, and talked first to Marge. "Jim said he has a bullet wound. Is that right?" Marge nodded. "Did the bullet go on through?"

Marge replied, "The one through his ear, yes. The one in his chest, no."

Dr. Chisholm looked at both Billy's ears. "This ear thing doesn't amount to much, but we have to try to get the bullet out of his chest."

Dr. Chisholm turned to Susan. "The bullet went up high enough it missed his heart, or he'd already be dead by now. His breathing seems normal, so maybe it missed his lung too. But we have to try to get the bullet out. Can we lay him on the kitchen table?" Susan nodded.

Dr. Chisholm turned to Mr. Crushman. "Get the family outside, then help me carry him into the kitchen and put him on the table."

Susan looked nauseous, but said, "I won't go outside. Billy's my husband, and I'll stay with him."

Jim Crushman answered, "It's gonna be gory and ugly. I'll walk out with you." He took her left hand, pulled, and Susan went. She beckoned to Mary Lynne and W.E. to follow.

Susan encouraged the children to lie down in the grass adjacent to the house, and to sleep if they could. They eventually slept, and Jim came back to the door about midnight. Jim's old face looked drained. He said, "He's alive, but we couldn't get the bullet. Doc said it's lodged against a rib by his back, and Billy might not walk again if he damaged the bones there. He's not sure Billy'll make it. The good thing is, he was out the entire time and didn't feel a thing."

Susan looked at her sleeping children, put on a resolute face, and said, "I'll go see him now." She brushed past a half-hearted effort by Crushman to stop her, looked at Billy, and cried more.

She recovered after a few minutes, and asked Dr. Chishom, "What are his chances?"

"Maybe about fifty-fifty." He started toward the door.

"Billy can't stay here on the table. Will you help Jim get him into his bed?"

Dr, Chisholm sighed, stopped, and answered, "Yeah, I'll help."

He did help, and started to leave again, but Marge asked him to look at Susan's hand. He did, and asked her, "How'd this happen?"

"Tim shot me."

"Tim?"

"I couldn't see his face, because of a hood, but he was so little, I know he was Tim."

"All I care about is that it's a gunshot wound, right?"

"Right."

Dr. Chisholm put a bandage on Susan's hand, and told her it would heal, but because it shattered a knuckle it would take months, and might leave a scar. He started again to leave, but Susan stopped him again. "What if Billy takes a turn for the worse. Will you check back out here in the morning?"

The doctor sighed again. "I've done all I can. The rest is up to him." He made it all the way to the door this time, and out to his horse. He rode to the driveway and disappeared behind the trees.

Susan went out and woke the children. W.E. asked, "Is Daddy all right?"

"Yes, honey, he'll be fine."

Mary Lynne asked, "Is he fine now?"

"Well, no, he's asleep now, but he'll wake up and play with you like he always did."

Mary Lynne cried but W.E. didn't. All three of them went in, stopped by Billy's bed, and Susan said, "Daddy's the main prayer person in our family, but he can't do it right now, so I think we should." They all bowed their heads and Susan prayed out loud, "*God, please be with Billy and with us. Please return the old original Billy to us. Amen.*

Susan took the children back to their bedrooms, then went to sit with Billy and to watch for a change in him. Near morning, Billy opened his eyes. Susan said, "I love you. How do you feel?"

Billy whispered, "I love you too. I feel awful." He closed his eyes again, but re-opened them about six o"clock. "What happened?"

Susan talked for many minutes, and gave him a complete account. He seemed to understand, and slowly improved for two days, then developed a fever the third day.

Susan sent Mary Lynne to get Marge again. Marge came in the house, touched Billy's forehead briefly, and said, "He has an infection. We need Dr. Chisholm out here again."

"I agree, but Dr. Chisholm said he wouldn't come again."

"Nonsense, child. I'll go for him myself. Can I ride your horse?" Susan sent W.E. to get Oskena into the barn. Marge said she could saddle her. She did, but returned about two hours later, when Billy's forehead felt even hotter than before. She reported, "Dr. Chisholm won't come. He said he has no medicine for an infection, and Billy'll have to fight it off himself."

Billy tried to fight it off, but lost. He died on Thursday, October twenty-eighth, 1915.

Susan tried to comfort the children, but she knew she couldn't. She couldn't even comfort herself. She asked Pastor Javier to make the funeral arrangements, because she didn't think she could do it. They held the funeral the following Wednesday. So many people attended the funeral that some had to stand outside in the light drizzle that began about an hour before. Susan remembered the people she saw before the funeral, but her mind faded out as the funeral went on, and she didn't even remember most conversations. She saw almost everyone she expected, and many she didn't. For example, Robert and Samantha from Strick, the Smithsons from Olathe and Edith Hastings from Humphrey attended; she had no idea how they even knew about Billy's death. She saw Ben Wilson and Gertie Knight; she expected one but not both, because she knew Sally's mind had gone completely. She sort of expected to see Ben Gibson, Sr., plus Dave, Lee, and Ben Jr.'s wife Lois, because Ben Jr. served as a pallbearer. But she didn't expect to see almost everybody Billy had built a building for earlier. She saw a few other people she didn't expect, like Sheriff Glosshart, Sheriff Everly, and Dr. Chisholm, but she did expect to see Sam and Jane Meskur, along with members of South Sinfe Church and the Baptist Church in Fiskur. She didn't see Tim Bolivan; she tried to recognize people she could regard as accomplices to Billy's murder, but could not. Gertie talked to her briefly after the funeral, but she didn't remember what they talked about. She gathered up her three children and walked home as soon as she thought it appropriate. She knew the children talked to her and she talked to them, but the details didn't stay in her mind. The next morning at breakfast, however, she talked to Mary Lynne and W.E.

"As soon as you two go to school, I plan to go to Riverbeach to talk to Sheriff Glosshart, and to stop on the way back to talk to Gertie Knight. W.E., can you get Oskena in the barn again? When you do, and as you and Mary Lynne leave for school, Janet and I will walk with you both to the road south, then Janet and I'll walk on to Marge's house. I'll ask her if Janet can stay with her all day, while I go to Riverbeach."

Six-year-old W.E. looked angry. "Why you going to Riverbeach? I can go too. I'm almost as old as Dad was when he took over for his dad. Me and Dad used to ride double on Oskena all the time."

Susan allowed a sad smile to briefly hover on her face. "Nevermind the why part. I know you're up to it, but so am I. I think I'll go alone this time, but you can go next time if you want."

Mary Lynne objected to the plan also. "Why do I have to go to school today? Why can't I wait until tomorrow? I don't wanna see anybody today."

Susan hugged her. "I know you don't, honey, and if I planned to be home, I wouldn't make you go. but you don't want to go to Marge's either do you?"

Neither W.E. nor Mary Lynne appeared happy with the plan, but eventually agreed to it.

When Susan returned from Marge's, she saddled Oskena, went to Riverbeach, and into the office of Sheriff Glosshart. The sheriff looked over his reading glasses when she opened the door, and said, "May I help you?"

"I'm Susa—"

"I know who you are. I was at Billy's funeral, remember? Please sit down."

"Yes, I remember. I came to tell you who shot him."

"You mean it wasn't an accident?"

"It most certainly was not."

"Who did it?"

"Tim Bolivan."

"You know that for sure?"

"Pretty close. He's the same little guy who's pestered us before, and has the same little voice. Billy knew him as Tim Bolivan, but he wore a sheet and a hood, so I couldn't see much except his small size."

"That's not enough for me to arrest him, but I'll snoop around a bit."

"I have his horse tied in my barn, plus his saddle." Susan stood, extended her hand, and the sheriff shook it. "Thank you sheriff. I'll appreciate whatever you can do." She went back out on the street, led Oskena to the edge of town, climbed on, and rode out to Ben Wilson's. She knocked on the door and Gertie Knight answered.

Susan smiled a tired smile. "Hello Gertie. Can I come in and talk to you a minute?"

"Of course, girl, get in here." Gertie reached out, seized Susan's shirt with both hands, and pulled her inside. They talked about Sally Wilson a minute or two, then Gertie asked, "What'd you come here to talk about?"

Susan cleared her throat and looked uncomfortable. "The farm. Billy thought he had to have it, but I can't run it, know nothing about it, and wondered if you'd take it back."

"I'd do almost anything for you, Susan, except that. I can't run it either, and don't know why I'd want it. But let's think about who might."

They sat in silence a few minutes, then briefly talked about possible buyers, ruled them out as prospects, and Susan left. She returned home and picked up Janet Sue before Mary Lynne and W.E. came home from school.

She continued to ponder who might buy the farms for a while, but Sheriff Glosshart rode in during the early evening to see the horse in the barn Susan mentioned. He went to the barn alone, didn't stay long, and rode out. He came back the next morning. He said, "I didn't realize you live in Joaquin County, but I don't have jurisdiction here. I'll work together with Sheriff Everly, and we'll get to the bottom of this, or my name's not Rick. One of us will probably be out here nearly every day for a while."

Sheriff Glosshart returned the very next day. He said, "I identified the horse as Tim's—that part was easy—and I found two of the sheeted men present the evening of the shooting willing to testify Tim did it. I hope he'll plead guilty; that would mean there won't be a real trial and you won't have to be present."

Thank you sheriff . . . I can't thank you enough. Billy would forgive Tim if he were alive, and let him off, but I want him out of Fiskur and stopped from ever doing anything like this again. So I really appreciate your work."

"I'll keep you updated on what happens." The sheriff rode back down the driveway. A couple months later, in January of the next year, he told Susan that Tim pled guilty to murder and received a sentence of 8 years in jail. He also agreed to never associate with the Ku Klux Klan again, and Sheriff Glosshart told Susan he'd watch for future evidence of Klan activity in Fiskur or anywhere in Sinfe County.

Susan called twelve-year-old Mary Lynne, six-year-old W.E., and two-year-old Janet Sue to a family meeting on a Tuesday in late January of 1916.

"I think all of you are too young to solely own farms, but I propose to take W.E. and Mary Lynne out of school tomorrow, so we can all go to Jaker, where we'll change the deeds on our farms. If you want to do it, we'll change the deed to the front thirty acres of the Thomas farm to be owned by W.E. and me jointly, the back ten to be owned by Janet Sue and me, the front thirty acres of the Knight farm to be owned by Mary Lynne and me, and the back ten acres by Janet Sue and me. We'll set it up so the titles will remain joint until each of you reach sixteen, then you will automatically become sole owner. Does that sound like a good plan to you guys?" The children all nodded yes, even Janet Sue.

Susan continued. "We'll need to find a renter to operate the farms for a while, because I can't do it. Jim Crushman agreed to do it this coming year, but we may need to find somebody else in later years. Jim said we can live here, keep our garden plot and our chickens as long as he rents the farms, but he'll manage all the rest. Is that all right?" The children nodded again. "Fine, then let's be ready to go when Mary Lynne normally starts for school. We'll take the horses and wagon if you'll drive, W.E."

W.E. grinned big. "Yep, I'll do it Momma." But then he frowned. "You said Daddy'd be fine. He's not."

"Yes, I said that, W.E., and shouldn't have. I was wrong."

"You prayed, and he died anyway. So what good did it do to pray?"

"Well, W.E., I asked Daddy exactly that same question when Robert died. Do you know what he said?"

W.E. appeared bored and looked away, but Mary Lynne asked, "What did he say?"

"He said God gives one of three answers to nearly every prayer. They are, 'No,' 'yes,' and 'wait.' I thought about what Daddy said, and decided God said both 'yes' and 'wait' to me about Robert. He said 'yes,' Robert will live with Me in heaven, but you have to 'wait' to see him until you're here too."

A flicker of interest crossed W.E.'s face early in Susan's talk, but died before Susan stopped. He said, "So if God said 'wait,' I don't see how that's different from 'no.'

Susan hesitated, then began again. "I said pretty close to that same thing to Daddy about Robert, and he said it was like you had asked if you could ride a race horse at the Joaquin County Fair. He told me he'd say 'wait,' because he thought you might get hurt, and he might continue to say it until you were old enough you didn't need his permission. But he said if you asked him to make a practice race track, and to buy a young colt you wanted to race later, and if you gentled the colt, practiced every day, and convinced him you knew how to do it, he'd say 'yes' much sooner."

"So how do I practice to make God say yes, Daddy can come back here?"

"You practice being a godly person, you think about how you can be a good Daddy yourself someday, and you convince God you'll be a good citizen of heaven some day."

"That doesn't make sense, Mom."

"Maybe it doesn't today, but someday it will. And as I've thought about the 'wait' answer, it seems almost like a 'yes.' If we think more about Robert and Daddy than about ourselves, then to know they're alive and happy and want to see us, is terribly close to a yes. But any time you have another question, W.E., just ask me. I want to answer as many of your questions, about anything whatever, as I can."

W.E. suddenly grinned ear to ear. "I think I'll go out and chase the horses into the barn so we'll be ready to go first thing in the morning."

CPSIA information can be obtained at www.ICGtesting.com
Printed in the USA
LVOW04s1142120115

422401LV00002B/5/P